Pecking Order

Pecking Order

Joy Berthoud

VICTOR GOLLANCZ
LONDON

First published in Great Britain 1996
by Victor Gollancz
An imprint of the Cassell Group
Wellington House, 125 Strand, London WC2R 0BB

A Gollancz Paperback Original

© Joy Berthoud 1996

The right of Joy Berthoud to be identified as author of
this work has been asserted by her in accordance with
the Copyright, Designs and Patents Act, 1988.

A catalogue record for this book is
available from the British Library.

ISBN 0 575 06035 2

Typeset by CentraCet, Cambridge.
Printed and bound by
Guernsey Press Co. Ltd, Guernsey, Channel Isles

99 98 97 96 10 9 8 7 6 5 4 3 2 1

With thanks for the help and support of my family, friends and those involved in the production of this book.

Contents

Introduction

Everyone has their place in the family. Everyone is a first child, a second child, an only child, a middle child, the youngest child – or perhaps the seventh child in a large family. Accordingly, we all have our position somewhere in the family pecking order.

As a consequence, no two children in the same family have quite the same experience of it. They see the family, and life, from a different perspective. This perspective – also known as birth order – is a key structural element of the formation of the personality Family fortunes may change, for better or worse; accidents may happen: our place in the family will be a factor in the way we react to such events and the influence they have on our lives. The family is a microcosm of society. It is where we learn to cope with life outside it. Relationships formed within the family will strongly affect the way we face the wider world – with self-confidence, or with feelings of inadequacy. The family is also about power and how to use, share, deflect and acquire it, as children are often alarmingly swift to understand. We carry with us into adult life the cumulative effects of our place in the family, of our sibling relationships and rivalries, on which our adult identity and relationships are based.

I was first struck by the full significance of family place or birth order when I was listening to my own daughters one day. The elder child was helping the younger with homework. 'Think, come on, *think!*' she shouted at her. About to intervene, I was suddenly struck by the similarities of this exchange to others a generation ago, when I used to help my younger sister with her homework. I began to make comparisons. My elder daughter and I are both bossy, achievers, conformist and conscientious; my sister and my younger daughter are risk-takers, emotional, open-minded and impulsive. All four of us are related, of course, and it is therefore likely that my children will have inherited some of the characteristics of members of my immediate family as well as some of my own. Yet I was interested that these traits should be repeated in the same sequence. The more people I talked to, the more reinforcement I found for my growing belief in the importance of birth order.

Alfred Adler, the Austrian psychiatrist and former disciple of Freud who pioneered the concept of the inferiority complex, felt that birth order and relationships with siblings provided the single most reliable predictor of human behaviour, even taking account of other non-genetic environmental influences such as social class, geographic origins and relations with parents. Other psychologists, notably James Bossard and Eleanor Boll, have underlined the importance of sibling relationships. Children in the same family, they point out, play together, work together and are likely to be together for long periods of time. They are, moreover, in very close contact: they bathe, sleep, dress, undress, argue together. Psychologically speaking, they say, siblings live with each other in the nude.

This book is intended to make accessible some of the research which has been done in this field; to illustrate through the experience of a cross-section of people of both sexes how birth order affects individual lives. Researchers have accepted that first-born children and those who arrive later have different characteristics. But in the case of non-first-born children, they have neglected to differentiate between the other places within the family pecking order (Koch, Rothbart and Sutton-Smith and Rosenberg are exceptions). Yet, as I hope this book will demonstrate, the difference, say, between the effects on a second child and those on the youngest can be considerable.

Here each chapter covers a place in the family – the first child, second child, only child, middle and youngest – plus the effects of birth order on twins, a child in a large family, an adopted child and a child in a step-family. There will be some overlap, for instance, in the case of the middle child of a large family. The book gives a general overview of the accepted research and wisdom relating to each family place, analysing its potential influence through the experiences of its incumbents, and drawing on the evidence provided by a number of writers, musicians, composers, artists, sportsmen, politicians, actresses, their families and their biographers.

It need hardly be said that we are dealing here with an inexact science. Often the conclusions of research are contradictory, and academic experts have been known to change their views on the relative significance of genetic and environmental factors. Few facts are universally accepted in the realm of behaviour, and so we are not faced with clearly delineated roles for heredity and environment (nature and nurture) in determining human behaviour. Their interaction is complex, and we are only just beginning to understand it. But the search for this understanding provides new opportunities for beginning to know ourselves better.

1   The First Child

It is a fallacy that children born of the same parents and brought up under the same roof are in a similar psychic situation. The world appears a different place if viewed from the different standpoints of the first- or last-born. The first-born child is the centre of family attention, a source of great pleasure and great anxiety to its parents. Its first steps, its first words and other achievements are loudly applauded. The world revolves around it, and it has the exclusive love of its parents. It feels secure in its little kingdom – king or queen of the castle, indeed. Given that the average family in the UK has two children, a high proportion of the population will be either a first or a second child.

Since the first-born will in its early life be the only child, first children have much in common with only children. The arrival of the second child and the subsequent 'dethronement' of this 'king/queen', the adored and worshipped 'only' child, can prove traumatic, particularly for a child under three years old. Freud noted in 1948 that 'it is of particular interest to observe the behaviour of small children up to the age of two or three or a little older towards their young brothers and sisters. I am quite seriously of the opinion that a child can form a just estimate of the setback he has to expect at the hands of the little stranger.'

The first-born does not, initially at least, have to compete with other children and tends to grow up in the parents' world and to adopt their attitudes and manners. But with the arrival of the second child he is ousted from this privileged position, thrown back into the ignominy of childhood, and must start striving for recognition. Of all the traumas a child can suffer, the most significant is the withdrawal, or threat of withdrawal, of love and approval from the parent. That threat can cause deep psychological scars, creating deficiencies that adults may spend the rest of their lives trying to make good.

It is rather like, as a family therapist suggested, a husband saying to his wife, 'Darling, I love you so much, and you are so wonderful, that I've decided to have another wife like you. It will be so nice for you to have someone to talk to when I'm not here.' When the new wife arrives, all the neighbours crowd round and praise her. 'Isn't she adorable? What a lovely smile. Just look at those eyes!' Not surprisingly, the first wife then wants to send the intruder away, or at the very least to hurt or diminish her. But the husband expresses surprise and says that the first wife must look after the new one and be friends with her. So it continues. Before long the husband is saying, 'Oh, darling, you have a lot of clothes you can't get into now. Do give them to the new wife. And by the way, don't make a fuss about her using your computer, you must share things with her.'

With the attention of the mother distracted by the second child, the first turns to the father. The rights of primogeniture in our society used to exploit this tendency by giving the eldest son the compensation of knowing that he would ultimately become 'king' again by inheriting the leadership of the family and its goods and tradition. But family traditions no longer have the same influence or attraction: a modern eldest son would not, for example, necessarily welcome the prospect of going into the family business.

Having turned to the father, the first-born may find that he is too busy to give the child the attention it needs, which will result in a feeling of rejection. The experience of loss of status gives the first-born an understanding of power and authority. And because of the special access to and identification with the parents, this is adopted as a personal characteristic. At the same time, ambition grows with the child striving to regain its rightful place. Almost every first-born wants to conquer the world, and many do. It has been reported that most astronauts are eldest children, and *Who's Who* is disproportionately full of professors, scientists, men of letters, physicians and eminent people who were a first child.

The first-born's is the most complex of all family places. Eldest children are shaped and influenced by adults, yet exercise both surrogate and actual power over younger siblings. It is a two-way process. First children tend to be keen to please adults and to emulate them. Thus they are rather conservative, highly responsible and prefer verbal to physical discussions. But they can also be domineering and controlling towards their subordinates.

William James, the founder of American psychology, is said to have written of his younger brother Henry, the novelist, 'His writing is over-refined and elaborate. He should cultivate a directness of style. Delicacy, subtlety and ingenuity will take care of themselves.'

Sue is in her thirties and a successful solicitor.

I'm aware of the theories on first-born children and objectively I probably conform to the stereotype. I was under pressure to achieve, to work hard. First-borns are expected to shine in some way, whether it's being the nicest kid on the block or in terms of doing something with their lives. It has a lot to do with the family set-up. If achievement is regarded as a major priority, it's hard to shake that off in later life.

She has a brother, Ben, just eighteen months younger, who was very naughty and to a certain extent indulged.

I grew up with people always saying, 'Susan's so responsible, she's so well-behaved.' Being the first-born made me independent and self-reliant, because Ben grabbed so much attention when he came along. I learned not to seek attention and to sort out my own problems. I led him and was very protective of him – I still am. He is now in film-making and still comes to me for advice. He's more impulsive and emotional, while I'm shrewder and a lot more measured.

Sue went to university in Sussex, a long way from her home in Lancashire, and Ben followed her there. 'I found it a bit difficult at first, but he'd been to visit me a few times and liked the place, so that was that. I actually think that we were born in the right order. He's a natural follower and I'm a natural leader. It works well, and somehow there's never been any jealousy or rivalry.'

Some people resist the idea that they might have certain identifiable characteristics because of their birth order. Yet as you talk to them it becomes clear to both sides that this is so. Roger is a case in point. At twenty-three, he is the eldest of three, with a younger sister of eighteen and brother of thirteen. Despite his protests, he seems to be a typical first-born achiever. A very good degree at Oxford in material science has been followed by a year with an aerospace company working on space research. Soon he goes back to Oxford to do a Ph.D. in a similar field. His father has been with Shell most of his working life, first as an engineer and then in management. His mother qualified as a psychologist, but never practised, preferring to look after her family full-time. This was necessary, since his parents did not believe in boarding schools and travelled around the world from post to post.

Although nothing specific was ever said, I always had the feeling that my parents expected me to look after my brother and sister, rather than to set an example to them. My mother was very anxious to avoid any kind of competition or comparisons. The trouble was, when they were younger they used to get on my nerves, probably because of the age gap. Now it's different, and I'm pleased to hear from my mother that my brother looks up to me and is really thrilled when he gets a letter from me.

And if, say, his sister rings in despair with a computer problem, he is soothing and ultra-patient in helping her. 'It's great being the eldest and it's nice that they respect me, but most of all I'm looking forward to having good relationships with them. They already have interesting minds and it will be good to be on the same mental wavelength.'

At first Roger didn't feel he had a tendency to control situations, but then he thought again and realized that he lived by his Filofax, and liked to plan things carefully. 'I like to fill my time to the maximum so that I can feel I've achieved a lot in the day, and if you don't plan, it's a shambles.' His future is well thought out, too. After the Ph.D., he wants to return to the space industry – 'or what's left of it' – or, failing that, perhaps go into consultancy or management, as his father did.

Psychologists point out that fathers can display hostility towards the first son, as illustrated many times in the Bible, for instance, Jacob's hatred for his eldest son, Reuben. Roger felt that there wasn't so much hostility from his father as a lack of things they had in common when he was younger. Now that he and his father see less of each other they have a much better rapport.

According to Bossard and Boll, every family identifies at least one of its siblings as the responsible type, the one who is looked up to, who assumes the direction or supervision of the others. Indeed, 'responsible' is the word used most frequently to describe these siblings, though words such as dutiful, bossy, drudge, leader and martyr also recur. These are different facets of the same trait, and the words chosen seem to relate chiefly to the way in which someone's feelings of responsibility are exercised. Most frequently it is the eldest or elder daughter who becomes to some degree a second mother to the younger children.

Margaret is the eldest of five children. Her father died when she was thirteen, soon after the youngest child, an afterthought, was born. Her beautiful mother had been spoiled by her husband, and the adolescent Margaret admired her enormously. 'She was everything I wanted to be, and I was a bit jealous, too.'

Although Margaret's father had made some provision for the family, their financial situation deteriorated swiftly and Margaret was soon forced to find herself a Saturday job as well as doing the shopping, washing and cooking for the family, for her mother had gone to pieces following her husband's death. Even when the mother started to recover, she refused to look for part-time work, saying she must look after her family. Yet she still left the bulk of the chores to Margaret, who remained loyal, a dutiful and responsible daughter. Despite the limitations the family put on her life, she accepted willingly all the demands made on her.

Margaret secured a trainee job with the BBC, which had good prospects if she worked hard, which she did. She was soon offered promotion, but since this would have involved moving to Bristol, she couldn't accept. By now the 'afterthought' was six years old and very demanding. Her mother had put on a lot of weight, started drinking and sat around all day. Although somewhat resentful, she felt that 'somebody had to look after the poor little mite'.

Margaret's siblings were not much help. The brother

below her, an adventurous type, had gone off to sea to avoid the situation at home. The next brother had chronic asthma and was always poorly. Her sister became a social worker and should have been able to give her support, but she married, when very young, a man who soon revealed himself to be a wife-beater.

Margaret began to feel rather bitter, particularly when she received a proposal of marriage from a boyfriend with whom she worked. The family, particularly her mother, had been very unwelcoming when the young man had been to visit, and now said they didn't like him. As Margaret realized later, it was pure selfishness, but at the time she was persuaded to turn him down.

Eventually, she became one of the BBC's top producers, and now has her own flat near Shepherd's Bush. But her first-born's sense of duty kept holding her back when the moment came to think of her own life.

I could have travelled a lot when I was younger. I was offered posts in America and a great opportunity to set up a link in Australia. And I do still regret not marrying. But although it's tempting to blame my family, any sacrifices I made were ultimately my own choice. I did achieve quite a lot in spite of their demands, and I could never have let them down – I would just have felt so guilty.

Margaret's mother, now in her eighties, is still demanding and still manages to make Margaret feel guilty enough to visit her every other weekend. 'Well, she's very lonely, and I feel I must.'

*

Some people positively relish being an eldest child, are aware of the advantages as well as the disadvantages, and make the most of them.

Hugh, a man in his fifties, is the eldest of four and clearly happy with his place in the family. His parents ran a large hotel in a small village in the Borders. His grandparents lived nearby and he feels that, as the first child and first grandchild, he was undoubtedly spoiled.

I was the apple of my mum's eye. There's a feeling of being special when you're the first. I remember my grandmother telling me that it would never be the same with the others, though obviously she would never have said that to them. And I understand it better since I've had my own children. The first has to be special: it doesn't mean that you love them less or more; it's simply that you only have a first child once. The next ones are magical too, but they can't be the same.

Hugh admits, however, that his parents were more careful with him and he didn't have nearly as much freedom as the youngest. 'I suppose I paved the way for the others. My parents just didn't know how far they could trust me, so someone always had to take me to the bus stop to catch the bus for school, for instance.' His father was sometimes a little strict with him, 'but again, I think he was probably just reacting to my mum. He wanted me to be a man, so he used to take me fishing with him which was a great treat. But he'd know the point where I started to get cold and hungry and he'd make us stay out just a little bit longer.'

Hugh was always a hard worker and very self-confident, and excelled at school. 'I'm used to coming first, even now, and I'm aware that the others were always under pressure because of me. I've done well in career terms and they've copped the backlash. You know the kind of thing: "Why can't you be more like your big brother?"' Perhaps because of this, he has always got on best with the youngest sibling, a girl, who was not compared to him quite as directly as the others. 'She was a bit of a pest. She used to follow me everywhere. She'd come and watch me fishing, or walk the dog with me. But I feel closer to her than the other two, a bit more protective, and because there was a bigger age gap, I wasn't rammed down her throat as much. She could probably take it, anyway.'

One of the most famous first-borns in the country is our own Queen. She may have been brought up in what is effectively another world from the rest of us, but it is one in which the perceived status of the eldest child is perhaps more marked than anywhere else. She has all the characteristics of her place in the family: she is reliable, responsible, very much aware of her duties and always plays by the rules. She was, of course, groomed for her royal role, but even so these qualities seem to come naturally to her.

In her recent biography of the Queen, Sarah Bradford says that the monarch's sister, Margaret, has by contrast been described as attention-seeking, capricious, extrovert and a risk-taker. She is four years younger than the Queen, who has always played the part of the protective elder sister. Even in the earliest photographs of them together, Elizabeth has her arm round her young sister in an almost maternal manner.

George VI may have been a reluctant king, but he was an enthusiastic and doting father. He and his wife created a very close, happy family atmosphere and he often referred to the family as 'us four'. A friend of the Queen's said she thought they were everything a family should be. With such a protected childhood, the two children grew up very much together despite the age difference. As a result, Elizabeth was relatively young for her age, while Margaret was precocious for hers.

Elizabeth was shy and a little self-conscious. She found it difficult to be natural and relaxed. Her sister was quite different: a former courtier is quoted in the Bradford biography as saying that the King used to be quite fascinated by this pretty little thing he had produced who found everything so easy.

The daughter of another courtier said that the King spoiled Margaret quite dreadfully. She was undoubtedly his favourite, partly perhaps because as a younger son himself he had felt he had lived in the shadow of his elder brother, Edward VII, and he did not want Margaret to suffer in the same way. She would be allowed to stay up for dinner, then keep her parents and everyone waiting while she listened to the end of a programme on the radio.

The only person who seemed to realize the effect this was having on Elizabeth was the royal nanny, Crawfie. She was so concerned that she would suggest discreetly to party hosts that Elizabeth should be asked on her own, in an attempt to separate the sisters a little. But Elizabeth liked to go with Margaret. She would say, 'Oh, it's much easier when Margaret's there. Everybody laughs at what Margaret says.'

Margaret, the centre of attention, the King's spoiled darling, was absolutely devastated when he died. At the time, Elizabeth wrote to a friend, 'Mummy and Margaret have the biggest grief to bear, for their future must seem very blank, while I have a job and a family to think of.'

Now that 'us four' had become 'us three', the headship of the family fell to Elizabeth, and she felt as responsible for her sister as she had done in the nursery. So she was overjoyed when Margaret married Tony Armstrong-Jones and did everything she could to help them – including contributing to the cost of larger accommodation when the children started to arrive. Elizabeth had always felt sympathy for her sister's lack of a clearly defined role in life: she understood that most of the wilfulness was really a futile beating of wings against a closed window.

The Queen was desperately sad when the marriage failed. She loved her sister, who seemed doomed never to find happiness, and she was incredibly fond of the children, who had spent many holidays with her at Windsor, Balmoral and Sandringham while their parents were away on official and unofficial trips.

Their relationship over the years was sustained with Elizabeth assuming the position of the responsible elder sister and Margaret that of the naughty girl who was always getting into scrapes. Margaret, no doubt subconsciously jealous of her sister, was not above cocking a snook at her. But Elizabeth, always maternally protective, would never hear a word of criticism of her. In return, Margaret gave Elizabeth total loyalty.

Now seventy, the Queen was recently described by Lord Donoghue, who worked in Downing Street as senior policy adviser to prime ministers Wilson and Callaghan, as: 'Almost the best monarch in our history ... She has all the qualities which are important in that job – honesty, integrity, dignity, reliability.'

A special first-born indeed, but nevertheless a true first-born.

As these examples demonstrate, this combination of emulation of the parents and a strong sense of responsibility in first-born children makes many of them high achievers. Barbara Hepworth, the sculptor, was the first of four children. She succeeded in a very difficult field – especially so for a woman. Hepworth had two sisters and a brother, and both she and her youngest sister went on to have triplets themselves. She was a typical number one, extremely hard-working as well as talented at school. She played the piano as ably as she drew, won an array of prizes and was very much the headmistress's pet, says Sally Festing in her biography, A *Life of Forms*.

Hepworth's father, whom she greatly admired, was a stern, determined, frugal and ambitious man; her mother, by contrast, was gregarious. Her father became chief surveyor for Yorkshire and helped form her love of landscape by taking her with him on his drives around the county, whose hills and valleys remained a great inspiration. She was, undoubtedly, her father's favourite. Yet for all his evident love and pride in her achievements she always felt she was never quite good enough. She tended to be anxious: probably she had the perfectionism

23

common among first-borns. In the very male world of
sculpture she continued to feel frustrated and perhaps
undervalued, and she was overshadowed by Henry
Moore.

Her first marriage, to the ultra-charming, multi-tal-
ented but feckless artist John Skeaping, could be seen as
a reaction to all that grim ambition. She proved much
too single-minded and serious for Skeaping, and the
marriage did not last. He was supplanted by Ben Nicholson, the father of the triplets, who looked remarkably
like Hepworth's own father, but proved to be a bit of a
restless womanizer. Nevertheless, the marriage survived,
more or less, for twenty years.

Hepworth was not very close to her siblings. Her
brother Tony became an engineer, but then rather went
to pieces. The pressure to succeed placed on him by his
father was probably too much for him. Her sister, Joan,
was very quiet and after her marriage seemed to disap-
pear from Barbara's life except for one four-month visit
to the family in Cornwall to help nurse one of the
triplets, who had osteomyelitis. Hepworth saw more of
her youngest sister, Elizabeth, whose husband, John
Summerson, she liked. Hepworth even held a party for
them at her studio in Hampstead when they got married.
Elizabeth was said to be the only one with a temper and
seems to have been able to stand up to the rather
domineering and strong-willed Barbara. When their
mother was ill, they combined forces: Elizabeth visited
her in the nursing home and Barbara bore the brunt of
the cost.

As she got older, Hepworth did become admired and
respected throughout the art world and a household

name, alongside her rival Henry Moore. Her death in a
fire in her studio was tragic and dramatic. She was alone
and it was assumed that it was caused by her habit of
smoking in bed, often after drinking and taking a
sleeping tablet.

In view of the qualities we have already looked at, it is
not altogether unexpected to find a politician who is a
first-born, but one in particular combines a large number
of the characteristics we often see in 'number ones'.

Cecil Parkinson provides a good example of the
successful self-made man. The abilities and personality
needed to achieve this are those often found in first-
borns, as we discover from his autobiography.

Parkinson was born in 1931 into a working-class family
who lived in Carnforth, Lancashire, a town dominated
by the railways on which his grandfather, father and
uncles all worked. His mother, who had been in service
until her marriage, produced first a son, Cecil, and
eighteen months later, a daughter, Norma. Parkinson's
education began at a church primary school and he was
one of only three pupils selected to take the Eleven Plus
exam to try for a place at the grammar school in
Lancaster, the nearest big town, which had a very good
academic and sporting reputation. He passed, and thus
began his ascent of the ladder to success.

The boys at the grammar school came from a wide
range of backgrounds but academic and sporting
achievements were great levellers. Thanks to the excel-
lent education he had received in Carnforth, Parkinson
was put in the A stream immediately, and was soon
elected form captain. As for sport, at fifteen he broke the

school 440yds record and a year later he was Victor Ludorum.

Coming from a small town where there was a feeling that the ordinary man was powerless to influence events, he felt frustrated and unhappy. As a typical first-born, he needed to have some control over his destiny, and this led him in 1947 to join the Labour Party, which he felt wanted to give people a say in decisions that affected their lives.

Parkinson's hard work, popularity and sporting excellence was rewarded by a state scholarship to Cambridge University. The scholarship covered tuition fees and he got a full grant, but he worked in the holidays to earn enough to live on. It was while he was at Cambridge that he became disillusioned with the Labour Party. Although he still regarded the Conservatives as the defenders of privilege, he was much affected by a meeting of the Cambridge Union at which Iain Macleod, much more reasonable and rational than he expected of a Tory, made Herbert Morrison seem inadequate and patronizing.

After two years reading English, Parkinson decided to switch to something that might help him find a job, so he turned to law for his final year, and after Cambridge, he qualified as an accountant. He went into business, where his career flourished, and eventually he became a Tory MP and a member of the Cabinet.

Married with three daughters, Parkinson resigned as Secretary of State for Trade and Industry after a heavily publicized extra-marital affair, but was reinstated as Secretary of State for Energy after four years by Margaret Thatcher.

As Cecil Parkinson says himself, few would have imagined that the son of a railwayman would commit a Conservative government to privatization of the railways; that the former treasurer of the Labour League of Youth in a small northern town would become the chairman of the Conservative Party; that someone who in an early stage of his life was a pacifist could have served in a war Cabinet. But then, Cecil Parkinson is one of those golden boys – a first-born who would have succeeded at anything.

Sport is another arena in which the determination of the eldest child can be seen. The cricketer Geoffrey Boycott has been described as complex, controversial, domineering and selfish, but he is also someone whose courage and brilliance have led many to consider him the greatest batsman of our time.

Boycott is the eldest of three sons. He was born in the Yorkshire mining village of Fitzwilliam in 1940. Mum was the driving force of the family: he may well take after her, for his father was a simple, easy-going man who spent most of his energies earning a decent living down the mine. In his autobiography, Boycott says of his father, with great affection and sadness, that 'he seemed to be almost permanently tired' in spite of being a big, powerful man.

The family lived in one of the many back-to-back terraced houses in the village, and the boys of the neighbourhood used to play cricket in the narrow lanes behind the houses with stumps chalked on the wall. The young Geoffrey badly wanted to learn to play properly, and with the help and encouragement of an uncle and aunt, he persuaded his parents to scrape together the money to send him to a Saturday-morning cricket clinic. They were very proud of him, but in later years rarely managed to get to see him play at the top level.

Boycott was nominated the outstanding all-rounder by the cricket clinic and won a Len Hutton bat in a national newspaper competition. Of his determination there could be no doubt: patiently he would spend hours practising a drill that the clinic coach, Johnny Lawrence, had shown him, which involved endless combat with a ball on a piece of string.

When Boycott was ten years old his father had a bad accident down the mine and suffered a broken back, broken pelvis and broken legs. 'The accident ruined his health and his life; it ruined *him*' says Boycott. This family setback deepened the eldest son's sense of responsibility. Geoffrey was very close to his brothers: Tony joined in most of his outings and escapades, and he was very protective of Peter, who was eight years younger.

Over the years Boycott acquired a reputation for being a loner and seemed to be constantly defending himself against the accusation that he thought only of himself rather than of the good of the teams for which he played. Certainly he's a very dominant and outspoken character who knows what he wants, as so many first-borns do. But equally, there is an uncertain and introspective side to his character that makes him wonder why people react to him as they do. Part of his 'loner' image might be due to the fact that he didn't want to go into the bar with the lads after a game, which would have given him an opportunity to explain the reasons why he did what he did. But he doesn't like beer, and all the post-mortems upset and confused him.

Boycott says of himself that he's a player of the old school, who believes in the pursuit of excellence: a first-born perfectionist speaking.

If you asked someone to guess Winston Churchill's place in the family, the chances are they would certainly say he was a first child – his leadership, conviction, domination and determination to succeed all point in that direction. And they would be right.

Born at Blenheim Palace in 1874, Churchill was, he says in his memoirs, 'a child of the Victorian era when the structure of our country seemed firmly set, when its position in trade and on the seas was unrivalled and when the realization of the greatness of our empire and of our duty to preserve it was ever growing stronger'.

From his father, Lord Randolph Churchill, he acquired the traditions of the English aristocracy, which echo those of the first-born: self-confidence and paternalism. Indeed, it could be said that in the wider context of society, the aristocracy were the 'first child' of the class system. In addition, from his American mother came a pioneering spirit, lack of pretence, hatred of snobbery and a belief in the powers of one's own star, all of which encouraged his ambition.

Churchill's parents had a busy social life, so he was often left in the care of his nanny, Mrs Everest, a warm, comfortable woman whom he called Woom, and who adored him. She was his main companion and friend – he once described her to his mother as 'in my mind associated more than anything else with home'. This was perhaps an admonishment to his parents, who neglected him quite severely.

Before Harrow Churchill went to prep schools in Ascot and Brighton, where he showed little aptitude for anything and was quite badly behaved. This could have been a result of what seemed to be the virtual abandonment of his parents. In the school holidays he and his younger brother Jack were either left at Blenheim with the servants or taken by them to seaside resorts such as Cromer, and Mrs Everest used to take Winston to her sister's home on the Isle of Wight. On one occasion when he was in the school hospital with concussion, he sent three letters to his mother asking her to come and see him, but she did not. Even his headmaster at Harrow had to write to his parents when they had still not visited their son after six months. This must have been painful, but undoubtedly it made him independent and quite tough. They might not have given him their time, but they did give him money – fifteen shillings a week, which was more than many people earned. As a result, he was smoking regularly by fifteen and at sixteen started drinking champagne.

After Harrow Churchill went into the army as a junior cavalry officer. He was only twenty-one when he suffered the first of the attacks of acute – sometimes almost suicidal – depression which pursued him for the rest of his life. He referred to it as his 'black dog', which came, uninvited, to sit on his shoulder. He found the only way to deal with these attacks was to drive himself to keep busy. The incessant activity for which he was famous, then, reflected his own inner tensions.

From his difficult childhood, Churchill emerged a

strong character: ambitious, egocentric, convinced he was cast in the same mould as his hero, Napoleon. He was very fond of his brother Jack, who had also gone into the army and had a successful, but not outstanding career. When they were children and played toy soldiers together, Winston always commanded the British army, while Jack led the native troops to inevitable defeat.

Churchill's long, illustrious career in politics was underpinned by a major theme of his thinking: the stability of society and the preservation of the existing order. In that, he conformed to pattern: first-borns are nearly always conservative, with a small c if not in their political allegiances like Winston Churchill (his early years as a Liberal apart). Indeed, Churchill was a rather extreme embodiment of the challenges and sufferings to which first-borns are exposed.

A broad pattern emerges clearly from the lives described in this chapter. The first-born starts with all the benefits of an only child in terms of parental attention, and the longer this period lasts, the more painful the resulting dethronement by the second child is likely to be. The determination to regain what the first-born sees as his or her rightful place will help sow the seeds of the ambition that so often characterizes first-borns in later life, especially perhaps from an entrepreneurial point of view.

That ambition is likely to be reinforced by parental pressure. For parents, the first child remains special, and they expect something special from him or her. This sense of being special can be a source of great confidence, but it can also leave the lingering feeling of not quite measuring up to expectations that seems to have

31

dogged Barbara Hepworth. Another potential risk, mainly for first-born daughters, is that a sense of loyalty and duty will create an obligation to support or stand in for an inadequate mother.

All in all, being the first is liable to increase the pressures on a child, but at the same time to help shape those qualities of character – determination, energy, sometimes perfectionism – required to meet the challenges of life. The result is very often a full and fulfilled life.

2   The Second Child

Sisters and brothers do not necessarily like each other, of course, but they certainly have a powerful and lasting impact on each other. They provide each other with experiences in sharing, in co-operating, in compromising. They force each other to confront and deal with the painful emotions of jealousy and greed. They enable each other to develop resources to deal with other difficult situations later in life.

Second children are far from isolated. There will be at least one other child around, and if that child is a popular one, there may be lots of other little visitors coming and going. Their parents' attention must be shared. Being the second child in a two-child family, like being the youngest in a larger family, means never knowing a privileged position or a feeling of superiority; never being the biggest, the best or the one who knows most. Things may even out later on, but the first few years can be disheartening. As one adult second-born put it, 'There's always someone half a lap ahead of you.' Life is a race against the odds.

This kind of sibling rivalry has a long, and sometimes tragic history. The first murder in the Old Testament involved Cain killing his brother Abel. Then Jacob, who hated being a second child, took the birthright from his older brother Esau.

If the first child becomes interested in 'learning' – and this is often the case, since parents have had more time to devote to helping him – the second child may feel squeezed out of the scholastic side of life. There is undoubtedly an 'academic primogeniture' in operation in most families. As the role of the family intellectual has already been taken, the second child may be encouraged to find something else to be good at. This may not be expressed in so many words but the message is clear nevertheless. This can be a self-fulfilling prophecy; in other cases, the feeling of inferiority can inspire the second child to outdo the first.

The international rugby player and former England captain Will Carling is the younger of two brothers. As their father was in the military and moved from post to post, the two boys were sent to boarding school from an early age. Will, naturally, leaned heavily on his brother Marcus, who was nineteen months older. He looked up to him as a kind of role model and they were, and still are, very close. Yet, as Peter Bills, Carling's biographer, observes, the need to match and if possible improve on his brother's successes sowed the seeds for dynamic achievement in the younger Carling. The inner drive for success has without doubt been an integral part of his development throughout his life.

As Adler tells us, often the line taken by the second-born is directly opposite to that chosen by the first. If the first child follows the father into the family business, then the rebel line might be an artistic one; in an artistic family, the second child might veer towards science or commerce. A second child will feel no respect for the established order because there is nothing to be gained from it – quite the reverse, in fact. If there's any subversion or revolution, it will be the second child who incites the other children to gang up against the authority of the first child or the parents.

Discouragement at the arrival of a second child may make the first behave badly. She might even begin to play the part of the baby, in order to become the centre of attention again. The second child will then try to shine by being just the opposite, and will grow up good, punctual, obedient and responsible. But in normal circumstances, it is the first child who feels happiest in authority, while the younger is more creative in opposition.

Originality and open-mindedness are just two of the characteristics we often see in the second child. And creativity and innovation lead on from these. Second-borns will also do their best to attract attention to themselves and yet underlying the dramas there are often feelings of inferiority and insecurity. Sometimes, reacting to the older sibling's caution and conservatism, they will be impulsive risk-takers.

The combative, rebellious spirit of the second child will, throughout life, be satisfied only by triumphing over authority, says Adler. Those who make laws or found institutions such as schools or religions are usually elder children, while younger children tend to preserve their childhood position by becoming critics or even revolutionaries. In George Eliot's *Middlemarch*, Dorothea, the elder of the two Brooke sisters, is reserved, intense, disciplined. Her younger sister Celia is described as having common sense and being amiable and worldly wise. George Eliot writes: 'Since Celia could remember, there had been a mixture of criticism and awe in her attitude towards her elder sister. The younger had always worn a yoke, but is there any yoked creature without its private opinions?'

Studies have shown that there is far more jealousy when two girls are born close together than between two boys. The following interview gives an insight into this relationship.

There were four children in the family, all born in India, where their father was an executive with an oil company. Their mother, a Cambridge graduate, had done a little coaching after university but in India she realized that it would be difficult to do any more than be her husband's wife.

The children arrived: first Sibyl; then, three years later, Ann; two years on John, and fourth and last, Amanda.

The problems started when Sibyl was sent away to stay with friends while her mother was in hospital having Ann. Just as Sibyl was about to come home, the monsoon started and delayed her return for some time. When she finally made it, her furious three-year-old stormed in, demanding to know, 'Where is that baby?' Fortunately, the baby was on the other side of the house, safe from the dethroned 'queen'. To placate Sybil, the new baby was fobbed off on to the ayah, and as a result, Ann's first language was the local Hindi dialect.

Not surprisingly, the relationship between the first and second daughters when young was, says Ann, 'very nervous, with a lot of jealousy. Sibyl was dazzlingly good at everything and my mother identified with her and rather ignored me. I didn't know how to deal with it so I just withdrew and became more and more silent.'

Their father travelled a great deal – at one time he was away for almost two years – and their mother grew more and more depressed and less interested in the family. 'She was never a warm and loving mother and, as my younger sister pointed out not long ago, the trouble was there just wasn't enough love to go round,' says Ann. When she was about seven, Ann's father came back from one of his trips and she suddenly realized that she could gain his attention by flirting with him. This alienated her mother even more. Sibyl hated her father and battled with him in the way an eldest son might have done.

The elder three children were sent off to school in England, spending their holidays in a boarding house on the coast. There was still intense competition between the two girls and Ann remembers an instance when she wrote and asked her mother if she could do Latin, and Sibyl 'absolutely freaked out'.

Sibyl had very little to do with the two younger ones, but Ann and John used to write to each other at their respective schools and as a result have remained very good friends. The youngest daughter, Amanda, was kept at home and seems to have avoided a bad relationship with anyone.

Ann does remember one friendly gesture Sibyl made when she was in her last year at school and Sibyl was in her last year at Cambridge. It obviously meant a lot to her. 'It was May Week and she invited me up and took me to parties and I met her friends. She knew I was apprehensive about Cambridge and she tried to reassure me. It was much appreciated.'

Through the years, the two girls have had many ups and downs which have on the whole brought them closer. There have been a few spats, but the only major one was when Ann married a very wealthy, artistic, intelligent, good-looking man. At the time, Sybil was short of money, trying to write with two small children at her feet and generally having a hard time. 'She said she thought I was far too unimaginative for him,' said Ann. The rivalry seems likely to continue, even into old age. But one feels that now there is an element of enjoyment in it.

Sibling rivalry is very common but it doesn't always occur. In some relationships the inherent characteristics of birth order can work very well.

Sally and Andrew have what might be seen as the ideal older brother–younger sister relationship, and one which also shows that the influence of an elder brother can be greater even than that of a father.

There are five years between them, and Sally remembers an almost idyllic childhood, playing games together in the garden with their father and long summer holidays in Cornwall with lots of scrambling about on rocks with bucketsful of 'finds'. 'Andy really was very good, looking back on it. I must have been a real pest, falling over and getting left behind. But he would always wait for me,' says Sally. Her brother even agreed to play dollies' tea parties with her, which was some concession at the self-conscious age of eight. 'He didn't seem to mind. On the other hand, he used to rob me blind of my share of Smarties.'

Andrew was very much a hero figure to her, and as Sally grew up, she tried to emulate him as much as possible. She was a tomboy and very good at sport, not at all a girly girl. Her mother was once heard to say: 'I always wanted a girl, and look what I got.'

Sally's mother, the wife of a brewery director and a Rotarian, played a traditional role in the family. 'She wanted to make me like her, so that she could control me,' says Sally. She was highly neurotic and began to have minor nervous breakdowns soon after Andy was sent to school on the Isle of Wight, some distance from home, at thirteen. Sally, who desperately missed her brother, bore the brunt of these breakdowns as she grew into her teens. Her brother used to come home occasionally at weekends and in the holidays, but he had become involved in the Scout movement and often went off with them to camp, or to stay with friends. As well as having to suffer her mother's bouts of depression, Sally also felt she was a pawn in her parents' deteriorating relationship. She left home as soon as she could.

Her brother continues to be very protective of her, even vetting her boyfriends. They see a lot of each other and are extremely close, particularly now that Sally has two small nieces. Sally feels that Andy is a typical first child and she a typical second, in that he has always played the system – 'Don't rock the boat' used to be one of his sayings, she remembers – whereas she has always fought it. She was one of the first in her group of friends to opt not to get married, but to live with her boyfriend, and became the only feminist among them.

Another initially less happy brother-and-sister relationship eventually did succeed extremely well. Heather is three years older than John and only now, in their late twenties, has any kind of balance been achieved in their relationship. Although John was the apple of his mother's eye, Heather was a very bright little girl. An early reader, clever with her hands, whether drawing or sewing, she was, said her teachers, always ready to try anything.

John's reaction to this was to be as mischievous as possible. He played endless tricks on his 'goody-goody' sister, like putting spiders in her bed. Sometimes there was a touch of malice in the teasing. He would, for example, destroy something she had spent hours doing or making, perhaps a picture or some dolls' clothes. This would, understandably, upset her a lot.

His parents would remonstrate with him about this behaviour. 'They used to talk about attention-seeking. I didn't know what that meant, but I could tell it wasn't good,' John recalls.

When I got older, I went in for coloured hair, black gear, all that stuff. It was a kind of rebellion, I suppose. I just wanted to do something different. My parents were shocked at first, but after a while they just ignored it.

I think my parents were quite even-handed, really. My father was away on business a lot and although my mother was very proud of my sister, she did make quite a fuss of me and I could always get round her.

So although John rebelled, he didn't feel rejected and develop the surliness that some rebellious younger siblings do. Instead, he became very laid back and easygoing, relaxed and popular with everyone, and left the ambition and drive to his sister. She did very well with her A-levels and went on to read languages at university.

As for John, their parents were told by his school to forget university, but after resitting one examination, he scraped high enough A-level grades to get a place at a 'new' university, albeit on a course which was not much in demand. After a year, though, he was able to change to a more interesting one. 'Then Dad got me a job in the vacation with a small market-research company, that was good fun,' he explains. 'I really enjoyed it, and they said they'd give me something permanent if I got my degree. So although I had a good time at university, I did quite a lot of work too.'

Today, John is working for one of the top advertising agencies. Meanwhile, Heather, having been offered a job with the European Union in Brussels when she left university, opted to get married instead. She is at home now, more than happy with her husband and children and doing some part-time translating. Her little brother, still as relaxed and charming as ever, says he feels he has almost caught up at last with his clever sister. They are obviously very fond of each other and John is a very popular uncle.

*

In some families, especially where there are only two children of the same sex, a second child who finds it difficult to compete or live up to parental expectations can react disastrously. The 1993 film *A River Runs Through It* told the story of a family in which the two sons conformed to first- and second-born types. It was, said a colleague, so like her own family.

The film was set in Montana, USA. The father of the family was a kind but strict Presbyterian minister whose hobby was fly-fishing. His two sons, about three years apart, also enjoyed the sport with him as youngsters.

The minister, a well-educated man, had great ambitions for his boys. The older one fulfilled these by becoming a university lecturer in the nearest big city. The younger had some difficulty with school work and eventually rejected it, becoming an expert fly-fisherman instead. His father was very proud of his son's skill, but soon realized that he was going to have to support him, perhaps for the rest of his life. Family rows became more and more frequent and ended with the younger son turning to drinking and gambling, and finally dying in a brothel brawl.

My colleague's two sons followed a similar pattern. There was pressure on them from their successful, rather authoritarian father to enter the professional world. The elder son, Peter, did well at school and went on to read law at university. He joined a large firm of solicitors in the City and one year later was poached by a much smaller firm who sent him to Germany, where he spent two years setting up a new office. A partnership offer seems likely soon.

Her younger son, Jamie, although as bright as his

brother, found life difficult at school, where he was constantly reminded of this paragon by his teachers. His parents tried to solve the problem by sending him to another school, but by then the damage was done. Now all he thought about was golf: his father had taught both boys to play on their local course in Dorset.

When Jamie left school, he spent every hour he could on the golf course, hoping that he might eventually become a professional. He worked in supermarkets, shelf-filling and cleaning floors, but never earned enough money to support himself. In desperation, his father put up the money for a share in the sports shop on the course to enable Jamie to run it. But it didn't do well, and having run out of credit there, he has been drifting round other courses hoping to find something to do.

Jamie had the same potential as his brother, but was overshadowed by him and then refused to even try to compete.

The typical traits of a second-born child, rebelliousness and creativity, could certainly be seen in the personality of Oscar Wilde.

The Wilde family lived in Dublin towards the end of the Victorian era. There were three children, Willie, Oscar, who was two years younger, and Isola, who was three years younger than Oscar. Isola died when she was only nine years old.

Their father, William, was an eminent eye and ear surgeon who was knighted for his work. He was vain, wiry and restless, a gregarious man who liked to dominate dinner tables. At nearly six feet, their mother, who wrote poetry, was taller than her husband and had a very strong personality. She wore dramatic, even eccentric clothes, and so usually made an effective entrance at any gathering. Although her name was Jane, she preferred to be called Speranza.

Oscar was close to his mother, but his brother Willie was undoubtedly a serious rival for her affections. She referred to Willie as 'tall and spiritual, with large eyes full of expression', whereas Oscar was 'a great, stout creature'. Nevertheless, Lady Wilde declared that for the first ten years of his life, she had treated Oscar as a daughter. Certainly a photograph of him, aged four, shows him wearing a dress. His mother was, however, given to exaggeration, and since she had a very attractive little daughter in Isola, it seems unlikely that this statement was made seriously.

Wilde's biographer, Richard Ellman, says that Willie was clever and popular but more serious than his younger brother. He and Oscar went to Trinity College, Dublin, and Willie then decided to study law at the Middle Temple in London. But he left after a few months and eventually made his career at the Irish Bar.

Oscar was a keen and talented classicist, and with the encouragement of his professor, successfully applied for a place at Oxford University. On his arrival at Madgalen College he embarked on a life which was in some ways a reaction to his brother's sensible, professional approach. Oscar wanted a life that was both aesthetic and unconventional. He had already begun to develop a flamboyance, wit and conversational brilliance which had made him stand out at Trinity. At Oxford and afterwards, his life became more and more outrageous. Ellman says that he declined in a quite public manner to live within his means, behave modestly, respect his elders or recognize nature and art in their accepted form. And yet at the same time he was the kindest of men and his quite beguiling charm always managed to temper his critics' ire.

In his third year Oscar spent his Easter vacation in Greece and was persuaded to stop off in Rome on the way home. He arrived back at Magdalen almost two weeks late and was rusticated until the October term. But he triumphed by being awarded the Newdigate Prize for poetry and achieving a double first. This pleased him, of course, but he always had the second child's relaxed attitude to success – if it didn't happen, a philosophical shrug of the shoulders would imply that it just wasn't meant to be.

Oxford was followed by a few years' lecturing in America, travelling in France and Italy, writing plays and poetry: the development of Wilde's life as an aesthete. But they were extravagant years in every way. So, at the instigation of his mother, and by then needing money and respectability, he married an intelligent, attractive, suitably well-heeled woman called Constance Lloyd. The marriage seemed happy and they had two sons, but Wilde continued to pursue his somewhat profligate lifestyle. The fatal meeting and subsequent love affair with Lord Alfred Douglas was the beginning of his downfall. Bosie, as Douglas was known, was spoiled, vain and a spendthrift. Oscar rapidly sank deeper and deeper into debt and his wife, family and many of his friends were alienated.

The doomed relationship led, eventually, to exposure, imprisonment and, after a few wretched years abroad, a tragic death in exile.

Often a second child becomes dependent on the first-born for family reasons – the parents' marriage break-up, for instance, or perhaps as a parental substitute when the children are sent away to school together. Eventually a kind of mutually supportive relationship is set up.

Charlie Chaplin's parents were music-hall entertainers. His father was a mimic and professional singer, his mother a singer too. His brother Sydney was four years older than Charlie and the two boys were looked after by their grandmother while their parents were touring the halls. When he was three and a half, Granny was taken to a mental home, largely incoherent and imagining mice and nettles in her bed. The parents' marriage broke up, and his mother worked all the hours she could to keep the family. Eventually she became ill, and at seven and eleven, Charlie and Sydney were sent to the Central London District Poor School at Hanwell, not returning home until two years later. Times were still hard and they were sent away again, this time to live with their errant father – until he died, aged thirty-seven, David Robinson, Chaplin's biographers, tells us.

By now the boys were, hardly surprisingly, very reliant on one another but Charlie was deprived, at least temporarily, of Sydney's protection when his brother was chosen for 'training for sea-service poor boys charge-able to metropolitan parishes and unions' and went off to sea. In the meantime, Charlie managed to join a troupe of boys known as the Eight Lancashire Lads. By the time Sydney came home, Charlie had a role in a play. By then he was fourteen, but still had difficulty reading, so Sydney read him the part until he was word-perfect. Sydney was then given a role in the same play and soon afterwards joined a comedy troupe which led to a place with Fred Karno's circus. He arranged an audition for Charlie, and they were soon working together again.

After a while, Sydney married a Karno actress and gave up the flat which had become more or less home to his younger brother. But by then Charlie was a little more established, and in a year or two he landed a contract to make films for Keystone in the US. Charlie was now twenty-four and kept Sydney up to date on his growing success by letter. By 1915, the big Charlie Chaplin boom was underway and Sydney had become his full-time business manager, a role he retained for most of Charlie's career. He dealt with all the negotiations while Charlie was being wooed on all sides and was fiercely protective during his many troubles with women and communist witch-hunters. The bond of understanding between them survived throughout their lives. Their aunt, Kate Mowbray, wrote:

It seems strange to me that anyone can write about Charlie Chaplin without mentioning his brother Sydney. They have been inseparable all their lives, except when fate intervened at intervals. Syd, of quiet manner, clever brain and steady nerve, has always looked after Charlie. Charlie always looked up to Syd, and Sydney would suffer anything to spare Charlie.

Sydney died, aged eighty, in Nice on Charlie's seventy-sixth birthday.

Two brothers who are very close, but totally different from each other, are the Sherrins. They enjoy each other's company, but happily accept that they live in different worlds. When they get together there's one topic that will always come up: cricket, which they both love.

The one thing you couldn't imagine Ned Sherrin doing is making hay on a farm in Somerset. The sophisticated, witty, showbiz personality with the rather camp manner conjures up an image of the archetypal urban man. Yet he and his elder brother Alfred were brought up on their father's farm in deepest Somerset, and help he did, with the haymaking and harvesting, albeit reluctantly, he told the *Sunday Times* magazine.

'My brother is a much more responsible person than I am and I honestly don't think he wanted anything else in life but to run the farm,' said Ned of Alfred.

I used to have to help out after school and in the holidays, but I spun out each job as long as possible and I was very good at remembering homework. When I first went to school I was known as 'Trailer' because of the way I used to follow my brother around. He never minded and was always very protective.

Alfred is a totally honest, straightforward, supportive, good, kind man. I'm not nearly as nice, nor as affectionate.

Ned obviously got on well with his mother, but he

says he thinks he was a fairly exotic creature as far as his father was concerned. Their mother came from a legal family – her father was a solicitor – and when it became apparent that farming was not for Ned, he was encouraged in that direction and did eventually qualify as a barrister. Alfred said of Ned:

> He was always very confident and so articulate that there was never any point in arguing with him. He went further academically than I did, and he is now as out of his depth in Somerset as I am in London. He was expected to help on the farm when he was at school, and he always did, but he managed to avoid jobs that meant getting covered in oil or grease. As boys, when I was playing with my Meccano, he was playing with a wooden theatre and acting all the parts. He was in all the school plays and has always been star of the show. He really is a great entertainer. He organized some of the productions as well.

Another first-born happy to stay out of the limelight while her more adventurous sister took the stage is Muriel, sister of Lady Thatcher.

Margaret Roberts was born two years after Muriel. The family lived in Grantham, where their father had a grocer's shop and was deeply involved in local government – he was mayor of Grantham for a year. Their mother was a professional dressmaker and also helped her husband in the shop. They were known in the town as a very hard-working, serious family, and were much respected. Margaret Wickstead, one of Lady Thatcher's contemporaries at school and at Oxford with her, said in a BBC interview that 'Mr Roberts was perhaps at one time the most respected Grantham citizen'.

The Roberts were strict Methodists and the two girls went to church three times on Sunday. Their life does not sound much fun, centring as it did on work, church and culture (Margaret played the piano well).

In her biography Penny Junor says that Muriel was conventional, not one for kicking away the traces. She was happy to go off to Birmingham at fifteen to train to be a physiotherapist. She would pass on clothes and accessories to Margaret, even when her sister was an MP and very clothes-conscious.

With Muriel's departure Margaret was in effect an 'only' at thirteen. Attention was therefore focused on her, particularly by her father. He recognized her potential and strongly encouraged her interest in politics. He had great ambitions for her, but although he was said to be authoritarian, he was a kindly man, not at all forbidding, and devoted to her. When she became prime minister, nine years after his death, she said, 'I owe almost everything to my father.' Of her mother, on the other hand: 'I loved her dearly, but after I was fifteen, we had nothing more to say to each other.'

Margaret distributed leaflets and canvassed for her father and learned as much as she could about local government procedures and elections. She was not at all shy or reserved as a young woman. Margaret Wickstead remembers this small, bright-eyed fourth-former standing up and asking a visiting lecturer, Bernard Newman, a question in almost parliamentary language. 'Does the speaker think so and so?' The sixth-formers were not amused.

At the Kesteven and Grantham Girls' School, Margaret was known as hard-working rather than clever. However, she got into Oxford to read chemistry, despite not having the obligatory Latin. She then compressed a five-year Latin course into a few months. At Oxford, she tended to irritate people by talking incessantly about what Daddy thought of this and that, and was very active in the Oxford University Conservative Association.

Margaret took her degree and got a second. Soon afterwards, Margaret Wickstead recalls, 'We were walking down past Rhodes House and she said, "You know, I've simply got to read law. It's no good, Margaret, chemistry is no good for politics. I shall set about reading law." And she did.'

Margaret was eventually called to the Bar in 1954, when she was twenty-nine, having earlier worked as a research chemist, married Denis Thatcher and given birth to twins. To the delight of her father, she was elected Conversative MP for Finchley in 1959, rising eventually to become a Cabinet minister, party leader and, in 1979, prime minister.

In her early days as an MP, Margaret and Muriel occasionally had lunch when Muriel was in town. As her life became busier, there was less and less time, even for her own family. But Muriel was very supportive. She had married a Scottish farmer but when their mother was dying of cancer, she came home and nursed her. In this we see another example of the sense of responsibility of the first-born.

To sum up, then, although first-borns are generally acknowledged to be the family's achievers, many second-borns are very successful because they try harder. The lives of Margaret Thatcher and Will Carling demonstrate this point. In other instances, and particularly between girls, there may be unpleasant sibling rivalry that can degenerate into corrosive jealousy. However, being born second more frequently prompts a rebellion against authority and against the example set by a striving elder sibling regarded as a paragon of virtue both at home and at school.

This reaction often takes the form of originality and creativity, Oscar Wilde being an extreme case in point. In other instances, it can lead to second-borns dropping out of the rat race and into a state of hopelessness that may be life-threatening. More frequently, number twos are merely late developers who nonetheless retain in later life the more laid-back attitudes that are, in a sense, their birthright.

3   The Middle Child

Sometimes known as the 'monkey in the middle', the middle child can have a difficult path to tread. Born into a world which already contains the first child, it is for a time the youngest, and may even challenge its older sibling, or siblings. But then, as happened earlier to the first-born, the middle child's view of the structure of the family is transformed by the birth of a further rival for parental affection: it now finds itself poised uneasily between the eldest and youngest, both of whom have a clear, unchallenged status.

Some middle children are able to maximize the opportunities for diverse relationships, using their experience within the family to develop skills of arbitration and negotiation. But others – and these tend to be in the majority – slip through the net and feel for most of their lives 'the odd one out', even overlooked or excluded. Their methods of protest vary, but are often attention-seeking – perhaps odd clothes or hair, or even strange behaviour. They often feel that they matter least among their siblings and sometimes tend towards depression, or even paranoia. As a result they may want to leave the family at an earlier age than their siblings. They may move out, move far away, or opt for a professional career quite different from that of the rest of the family.

In Jon Cook's study of sibling rivalry mothers reported

that the most difficult behaviour came from the middle child in the family. This was attributed to a struggle for identity and maternal attention in an environment where a certain status is attached to being the eldest and where the mother tends to favour the youngest child. In one case, when a middle sister was asked to look after her little brother, her older sister always pushed her out of the way and said, 'I'll do it.' Then, of course, her mother blamed her for not looking after the baby.

However, the situation can be very different when the middle child is of a different sex from the others – a boy with two sisters or a girl with four brothers. Then they tend to be treasured and cared for by siblings and parents alike. The intensity of the middle child's feelings will therefore naturally vary from family to family, depending to some extent on such gender and age-gap factors. But the Macleans are fairly typical of an apparently happy, well-adjusted family which ran into some difficulties.

Ruth, the eldest girl, was always cool, detached and much admired as well as loved, though sometimes rather daunting and judgemental. She was highly intelligent, did very well at school, and eventually became a doctor. The second daughter, Liz, was a cuddly baby and an intelligent, lively and amusing young girl, displaying many of the traits of the second-born. But when Harry, the hoped-for son, arrived, she began to feel left out, a feeling that continued for years. Pushed out, as she saw it, by Harry, she constantly demanded attention. Her mother says that although Harry was the baby, in family photographs she is always carrying Liz while someone else is holding Harry. Sometimes Liz drew attention to herself by her behaviour – early smoking and the like – sometimes by wearing eccentric clothes.

At school, Ruth was sensitive to her environment and always popular. Liz tried hard, but never managed to pick up what she was meant to do. She felt she couldn't compete, so she decided not to try and became quite rebellious. It was consistent with this behaviour that she opted not to go to university, and switched from one career to another, eventually ending up helping to run a desktop publishing company, which did very well.

The two girls were never close as sisters. Their mother once heard screams coming from the bathroom and found that Ruth had gone in and hit Liz with a very hard plastic duck. In spite of the blood running down Liz's face, Ruth said defiantly: 'I'm not sorry at all.'

Harry was always loving, affectionate and, with two overwhelming, bossy sisters, not surprisingly a late developer. However, although he and Liz had terrible fights occasionally, they were closer and had a much better relationship than did Ruth and Liz. Both Liz and Harry felt that Ruth pushed them away.

Ruth is now married with children, Liz is in a relationship in France and Harry is in Australia. When there is a family gathering everyone gets on very well together, but otherwise there is still little communication between Ruth and Liz. Harry and Liz, by contrast, are often in touch, in spite of the geographical distance between them.

Some middle children seem to have the odds stacked even more heavily against them.

Tom is the elder of non-identical twins, but in his case, being the middle child has been more significant than being a twin. Not only is Tom's brother, who is older by two years, cleverer, more athletic and better-looking than he is, but his twin sister is taller than he is and, at sixteen, already a beauty.

Tom hasn't always been the odd man out. Usually the elder twin is bigger, healthier and the more dominant of the two, and initially this was so in his case. But his sister Pamela shot up when she was nine years old and, as so often happens with girls, was soon ahead of him at school as well, not to mention becoming pretty.

Tom comes from what seems a well-balanced family. His father is successful and ambitious for his children. The elder son, Nick, is a chip off the old block: having flourished at the local primary, he was accepted at one of the most academic schools in the country and has recently won a scholarship to Oxford. Like his father, Nick is large and athletic. Also like his father, he has a rather patronizing attitude to Tom.

Their mother, however, is gentle and caring and complements her husband well. Realizing that Tom was suffering, she became almost over-protective. When he was unhappy at school, she swiftly removed him and sent him to another, then another. For a year or so, he more or less dropped out and there was a real fear that he had become seriously involved in the drugs scene. Whether or not that was the case, he is now putting together a portfolio of drawings, life studies and collages, and has a good chance of a place on an art foundation course. With luck that will lead to full-time studies at art college.

Tom gets on well with his twin and they have many friends in common. But although she and Nick are good friends, 'Tom and Nick are so like chalk and cheese, they will never have anything in common,' says their mother sadly.

An item on the Radio 4 programme *The Afternoon Shift* about middle children elicited some revealing thoughts and feelings.

One of those who took part was Jenny. With an older sister and a younger brother, both barristers, she 'opted for stupidity', she says. In fact she became a successful comedienne and well-adjusted mother and feels, with hindsight, that she is less uptight and more sociable than her older sister. 'As a mother, I know now that you face your first child in fear and horror, but with the second, you are a lot slobbier and more relaxed,' she says.

Jenny comes from an army family and admits she had 'an Enid Blyton and Clarks' sandals childhood', quite idyllic. Her sister was naturally bright and became head girl at school. She went to the same grammar school, but was so much in her sister's shadow that all she could do was behave like 'a slapper from hell', tie her school shirt under her 'non-existent bosom' and 'swear a lot'. She says: 'My sister's room was always neat and tidy with pants in the right drawer, while mine was like a pigsty.'

One of the constant complaints of the middle child, particularly girls, is that you never get anything new – you're always stuck with hand-me-downs. 'Well, I solved that one by getting so fat that nothing fitted me,' said Jenny triumphantly.

'But before all that, we had been invaded by the much-wanted sickly boy child. Why is it that the boy child is always much wanted?' she asked rhetorically. He also turned out to be incredibly bright and that was when, Jenny reckons, she gave up on the scholastic front. Trying to keep up with her sister was one thing, but having to fight a rearguard action at the same time was too much.

Ian was another sufferer. 'Not only was my brother head boy,' he recalled, 'but he was also the First King in the nativity play, in a red ermine cloak, while I was the shepherd boy with a tea towel on my head.'

Ian, the middle of three brothers, is a field officer for the National Canine League. His brothers, he says, are both 'in the professions', very conventional and very sporty. He found he couldn't compete and tried every form of protest when he was young, 'from drugs to rock 'n' roll'. 'I think I had my mid-life crisis when I was about twenty-four,' he says with a laugh. 'I suppose you could say that my elder brother did a certain amount of ground-breaking, but as I didn't particularly want to go and play cricket every weekend, it wasn't much use to me.' The one area where Ian excels is trichological. Both his brothers suffer from hereditary baldness, while his hair is thick and lustrous. To emphasize the point, he wears it long and flowing over his shoulders. He loves animals and is happy in his job. Whether his long-term future lies in this field, he is not sure. Worrying about career paths is in any case not his style.

Although Mark is the fourth of six brothers he is essentially another middle child. He is a DJ on weekend Radio 1 and explains:

In our culture, if you are a first-born African, your mother takes your name. My eldest brother is Michael, so she calls herself Mai (mother) Michael. It gives a strong feeling of identity. If my brother moved away, the next brother would move up and if I were the oldest one at home she would become 'Maimark'.

Of course, being fourth, you haven't a chance, and by the time they got to me, they wanted a girl anyway. There was massive pressure to conform on the career front. My eldest brother is a computer analyst, the next a Eurobond dealer, then a foreign-exchange dealer, then me. After me is an accountant and a civil engineer.

My father wanted me to do a course that would survive Armageddon, like being a doctor or a lawyer. So I did architecture for four years, then I gave up. I was wasting my life. I started writing and studying music. I was definitely rebelling; I did it partly because it was different, but also because I enjoy it.

He is now in a field he likes and excels in, and doesn't at all mind being the odd one out.

Damon Hill, motor-racing champion and son of Graham Hill, has one sister, Brigitte, who is two years older, and another, Samantha, four years younger.

He is ultra-competitive, determined and somewhat insular: all valuable qualities when the goal is to beat the opposition and become champion. Certainly it has taken determination to go after the mantle of his father Graham, twice world champion, who was killed in a plane crash in 1975. Damon was then fifteen, and it took the family a long time to recover, both emotionally and financially. His father had not made any provision for them, and his mother, Bette, had a hard time bringing up the three children on what was left after their large house in Hertfordshire was sold. She found a job to supplement the family income, but life was difficult for a few years.

Damon admits that until his father was killed, he had been a brat, playing up his mother for all he was worth. He says he got away with murder. 'When she was in hospital having Samantha, I refused to go to school. It took four neighbours to drag me screaming into a car.'

His sister Brigitte remembers the time when their mother came home with Samantha. 'He thought we didn't love him any more. He wouldn't look at Mummy and his bottom lip was trembling because he felt he was being replaced.'

Damon has both friends and enemies in the motor-racing world: those who say he is devious and awkward, and those who say he is kind and generous. Now in his mid-thirties, he has after many years of stubborn crusading more than established himself in the Formula 1 racing world.

Family circumstances forced Cindy Crawford, a middle child with two sisters, to become independent at an early age and she is regarded as an expert negotiator. She has now been a top international model for over ten years. Cindy was born in De Kalb, Illinois, just over thirty years ago, to Dan Crawford, an electrician, and his wife

Jennifer, who works at a bank during the week and as a sales assistant at the weekend.

Her older sister, Chris, is a computer consultant, and her younger sister, Danielle, a Peace Corps volunteer. Her parents divorced when she was fifteen and she was forced to take on more responsibilities than the average teenager. 'My mom was so wrapped up in taking care of herself. At fifteen I was an adult. I made my own money. I set my own curfew,' Cindy said in an interview with *GQ* magazine.

She spent three summers during high school detasselling corn in the fields around De Kalb, a job she has described as 'backbreaking sweaty monkey work'. Despite having to share family duties with her mother, Cindy excelled at school. When she was fourteen, she bet her father $200 that she would achieve straight As throughout her high-school career. Upon receiving her final report card, she collected her money. After she graduated from De Kalb High School, top of her class of course, she enrolled at Northwestern University, Illinois, where she studied chemical engineering on a full scholarship. During her single semester there, she encountered for perhaps the first time an attitude which would dog her for years: because she was beautiful she must be stupid. In the *GQ* interview, she recalls how, when she completed all the questions on her exam paper, the professor accused her of cheating. The accusation was, she believed, based on her score and her looks. When she did equally well in the final exam, he realized that she really did know her calculus.

There's a definite tendency for middle children to be

loners. Perhaps because they are betwixt and between, they feel a need to go off and do their own thing.

Cindy Crawford appeared in a Clairol hair show in Chicago, for fun, she says, and it led to modelling engagements all over the world. Her exclusive contract with Revlon was a multi-million-dollar deal. She attributes her success to her efficiency. She is very professional: many girls, she says, don't like to work with her because she's too businesslike. She arrives at nine because she wants to leave at five, doesn't go to work with bags under her eyes and never has chipped fingernails. If a photographer isn't doing his job properly, she'll tell him what to do: after all, if she looks bad in a photograph, they won't blame the photographer, they'll blame her. Here is a woman who is in control – as far as anyone can be – of her life.

Robert Graves, the writer and poet, had four brothers and sisters of his own and five half-brothers and -sisters from his father's first marriage.

His father, Alfred Perceval, was the son of the Anglican Bishop of Limerick. He married Jane Cooper, a laughing, lighthearted woman, when he was twenty-nine. She died of consumption eleven years later. Although he had loved her deeply, five years of coping with five children led him to marry Robert Graves' mother, a woman of altogether different clay. This was no love match, says his biographer, Martin Seymour-Smith.

Graves said that his mother, Amalia von Ranke, a ferocious religious evangelist, regarded marriage to his father as a good opportunity to do 'mission work in the field'. Seymour-Smith points out that many of the poet and novelist's less attractive features are attributable to his mother: her thoughtless and sometimes cruel piety became male priggishness in him. Nonetheless, throughout his life Graves remained extremely attached to her. His parents left Ireland and settled in Wimbledon a year before he was born. There were two sisters before Robert – Clarissa, who became an artist, and Rosaleen, who became a doctor. Just as Amalia was about to come home from hospital with Charles, his new brother, Robert developed scarlet fever and was immediately whisked into hospital. He was not allowed to come home for two months in case he infected the baby. So not only had he been banished from his home and loved ones by the newcomer, but also ousted from his position as the youngest child and only boy.

Soon after Charles came John. Charles grew up to be a journalist and John a headmaster. Robert seemed to have nothing in common with his sisters and disliked his brothers intensely. He was the non-conformist of the family. School was a disaster: at Charterhouse, his middle name, Von Ranke, was discovered, and with anti-German feeling rampant at the time, he had to feign madness to escape the campaign against him. After school he experienced the horror of the trenches of the First World War and was severely wounded after many desperate months. The shell-shock he suffered was to recur from time to time, but at least he was out of the war.

He married Nancy Nicholson, sister of the painter Ben Nicholson, with whom he had four children. For a few years the marriage was happy. By this time he had written something like fifty poems and had earned himself a reputation as an interesting minor poet. But eventually the stresses produced by his failure to support himself and his family by his writing began to affect his relationship with Nancy and she herself was often ill with worry. Just when they seemed to have reached a crisis, Graves was offered a professorship at Cairo University for three years. He and Nancy, with the children and their nurse, left for Cairo in January 1926. They were accompanied by Laura Riding, an American poet, who was an admirer of Graves' poetry and was to collaborate on a book with him.

Laura, who was to become his muse, was a very strong-minded woman, reminiscent of his mother perhaps. Indeed, she dominated the remainder of his life. Her literary influence and support transformed his attitude to writing, but their work together destroyed his marriage. He became obsessed with Laura, and eventually they both died within months of each other.

Graves has had a mixed reception from his readers. Some think he is an outstanding poet, others that he is overrated. Certainly his own ambivalence as a middle child is at times reflected in his work.

Another middle child from a large family, Edward Elgar, seems to have suffered somewhat from the paranoia that can affect middle children. He was born in 1857, the fourth and middle child of a piano-tuner, William, and his wife Anne. William also played the organ and the violin and later sold sheet music and instruments from a shop in Worcester. It was, in short, a modest background. There was Harry, Lucy, Polly then Edward, who was followed by Joe, Frank and Helen. His biographer, De-la-Noy, observes that pretty Polly was his favourite.

Harry died of scarlet fever when he was thirteen and two years later Joe died too. This double loss as a child, and the change in the balance of the family (although it left Edward still the middle child), must have put him under considerable pressure. Whatever the cause, he grew up to be a very repressed man. At thirty-two he married Caroline Roberts, eight years his senior and also his social superior. She devoted her life to supporting and promoting him and his career.

Caroline mollycoddled him: when he said he had a slight chill, she sent him to bed with seven hot-water bottles. It is hardly surprising that he became very difficult – moody, preoccupied with his health, short-tempered, prone to dramatization, self-pity and gross exaggeration. He alternated between being very kind, charming and even witty and considerable coldness.

In spite of his wife's kindness to him, Elgar kept his most overt expressions of emotional involvement for his male friends, though he liked to have flirtatious friendships with upper-class, good-looking women. Like many middle children, he was prone to depression and despair, though in his case these afflictions tended to be exaggerated. After one display of boorishness, Siegfried Sassoon said: 'There is no doubt Elgar is a very self-centred and inconsiderate man.' Above all, he was emotionally immature – yet he could write music in which so much emotion was distilled.

Elgar seems to have had little contact with his siblings, with the exception of Polly, later in life. His brother Frank had taken over his father's business and Helen became a mother superior in the Dominican Order. Even at the end, when he was garlanded with the OM, three knighthoods, a baronetcy and many foreign honours, Elgar was apt to suggest that he had not received much support, and despite his own modest upbringing, he had little sympathy for those who had struggled up without the aid of a relatively well-off wife.

As we have seen, being a middle child is not easy, whatever the size of the family. First you are ousted from your position as the youngest, then you are stuck between either two siblings, or two groups of siblings, who enjoy the status of oldest and youngest. Inevitably, therefore, middle children often seem to be seeking a role, a quest which may act as a spur to achievement. Yet even when they do carve out a position for themselves, as Elgar triumphantly did, they may be temperamentally unable to savour the fruits of their labours.

4 The Youngest Child

To be – and to remain – the youngest child is to have a position of considerable significance. The youngest is spared the trauma of dethronement. He can turn his whole attention forward: with no one behind him, he shoots ahead at a great pace to catch up with and even overtake older sisters and brothers. It is often youngest children, as well as the eldest, who accomplish great deeds. Their older siblings have paved the way so they have more self-confidence and are more adventurous. Even in fairy tales, we find Hans Andersen's Little Mermaid, the youngest of six sisters, is the only one who dared to venture into the human world. Shakespeare portrays the courageous Cordelia, King Lear's youngest daughter, as bravely insisting on honesty because she loves her father, unlike her hypocritical and greedy sisters.

Parents are much more relaxed with their baby, and sometimes a little sad if they know he is to be their last child. If there are several children in the family, the older children will help – usually willingly, since the youngest is nearly always adored by the others. Often there is a bond between the eldest and the youngest. This is particularly true if the eldest child is a girl, who may take on a surrogate mother's role, but the eldest brother, too, can feel very protective towards the family's youngest member.

The tendency of the youngest is not so much to tilt against authority as to outshine the whole world. He is the Hop o' my Thumb who puts on the giant's boots and outruns all the others. His goal is high and his failures and successes may be dramatic. If he succeeds, he may even be the first to leave the home and earn his living. His success is not burdened with the authoritarian and bitter attitudes that sometimes accompany the eldest through life, nor with the rebellious and discontented attitude of the second child.

Joseph is the best biblical illustration of such a character. Technically, he had a younger brother, Benjamin, but having left the family circle early he never knew him and remained psychologically the youngest. Joseph's dream of the ears of corn bowing down before his ear of corn shows both the striving of such a child to outdo the whole family and also the peculiarly gracious form that such efforts can take. Although the ears of corn of his father and his brothers must bow before his ear, the corn itself does not represent a wish to dominate but is a symbol of his desire to excel by becoming more fruitful than them, a dream that he was later to fulfil when he saved the land of Egypt from famine.

But just as the youngest child can flourish and contribute in notable ways, he can fail no less strikingly. It happens frequently that a youngest child is so pampered by her parents and older brothers and sisters that her direction and ambition is undermined. The family regard her as the smallest and the weakest. The child becomes so accustomed to this image of helplessness that she clings to it as an adult. She is so used to being spoiled and supported by others that she finds herself incapable of coping with life on her own.

Youngest children are also prone to feeling left out or even excluded. This is usually the result of jealousy. The nickname Tail-End Charlie is sometimes used to tease the baby of the family.

There is an American story which illustrates how this attitude can be carried into adulthood. Larry's sister baked him some Christmas cookies and gave them to his older brother to give to Larry. Larry recalls:

My brother got to my house, and before he gave me the box of cookies, he opened it up, looked inside, saw one cookie in the shape of an airplane, popped it into his mouth, and then pushed the box toward me. I was instantly eight years old. Here was my older brother taking my things *as usual*. I grabbed the box, hugged it to my chest and screamed, 'Those are my cookies! Linda gave them to *me!*' My brother looked at me, smiled, and said the same thing he always said: 'Oh yeah? What are you gonna do about it?'

Larry is close to fifty and his brother is approaching sixty.

On the whole, youngest children are happy, confident and well-adjusted, which makes them easy to live with. They usually want to prove they are as good as their older siblings, and as long as their ambition has not been undermined by being over-adored, they often do manage to outshine everyone else. Having had their way most of their lives, they expect and nearly always get it.

This is in no small way due to their easy-going charm and general affability.

My first interviewee is in many ways a typical youngest child, a happy person who has faced and dealt with her problems in a down-to-earth way.

Marcia was the youngest of five girls. When she was born her sisters were respectively thirteen, twelve, eight and two. So the family, as so often, was divided into three groups – the two older ones, the one in the middle, and the two little ones. The girl in the middle, Prue, had a chip on her shoulder, says Marcia, and the little ones she had to look after desperately tried to win her approval. But she was a loner and didn't really want to get involved with them. The next sister up also tended to keep to herself, but the eldest, Anne, was always delighted to see Marcia and made a great fuss of her.

Marcia agrees that she was probably spoiled, but she thoroughly enjoyed it and since, as she says, she didn't ask to be spoiled, she feels it wasn't any fault of hers. But as she grew up she found it frustrating that as the baby of the family, there was nothing she could do first: everything had been done already. Yet it was a very happy family and, on the whole, her sisters were very kind and loving and looked after her. She was closer to her mother than to her father, but she got on well with him. 'He was a great hugger,' she says.

She grew up and married and had an enormous desire to have a large family, like her own, but because of an infection, she was able to have only one child. She is very much aware of the only-child syndrome, but says her son seems a very well-balanced, intelligent boy and because she was spoiled herself she knows the things to do and those not to do.

She is an obviously happy person, relaxed, outgoing and friendly, with, apparently, few real problems. She was a naval wife for many years, which taught her a lot about living and managing on her own, and she has since written a bestseller about these experiences. As a result, she was interviewed on a local radio station and found to be such a natural communicator that they asked her if she would like her own chat show. Now she is a local radio star.

Youngest children can be at risk of being over-indulged. In Dorothy's case, it was fortunate that someone from outside the family who could see her situation in perspective was on hand to set her on the right path. Dorothy was the youngest of seven, with three sisters and three brothers, always doted on, spoiled even, though the family was relatively poor. When she was only six months old, her father was killed when he was thrown by a horse at the stables where he worked in Newmarket. Her mother, daunted by the task of bringing up her large family on very little money and no other support, moved to the outskirts of London, to be nearer a possible job market and to her older brother.

The eldest son, who had just gone to university, had to abandon his degree course and find a job. The next two girls, who were sixteen and eighteen, did not leave school, but found part-time jobs. The next child, a boy, went to the local grammar school and another went to the local primary school. This left two at home, a girl of nearly five and Dorothy, now nine months old.

Their mother managed to get a job supply teaching and the two older girls had to help look after the rest of the family. Dorothy admits that as she grew up she used her status as the youngest to manipulate her brothers and sisters. Often she would pretend she couldn't do something, like her homework or, when it was her turn, the hoovering, because she knew somebody would say, 'Here, I'll help you.' She was a very bright, happy little thing, always singing and laughing, and the others made a great pet of her.

Her mother, as a teacher, expected high standards from the children who were still at school and she noticed that Dorothy's school work was beginning to fall off. However, since Dorothy got into the grammar school, she said nothing. Dorothy was very popular at school. She was very easy-going and didn't take anything too seriously, including her work. She did badly in her O-levels and her mother was very upset, but the rest of the family urged their mother not to be too hard on her – 'She's just the baby.'

At about this time, Dorothy started going out with Nick, a boy in the year above her. He was good-looking and a great sportsman but also serious about his studies – he wanted to be a doctor. Her new boyfriend couldn't understand how such an intelligent girl could fail so many O-levels – until he met her family. Then he told her it was time she stopped opting out by being 'the baby' and grew up. If she didn't take responsibility for her own life, she was going to go on failing and her family wouldn't always be able to pick up the pieces. Well, that was the end of Nick.

But then Dorothy began to feel more and more that

there was some truth in what he had said. Her mother, when consulted, was immensely relieved. She realized that someone outside the family had managed to convey something that, had it come from within, would have looked like rejection.

Dorothy at last began to work hard and managed in a short time to make up lost ground. When she decided to study medicine, she had no difficulty in being accepted by a teaching hospital.

Hilary was doted on too, but in her case it proved to be an encouragement. She knew the direction in which she wanted to go, and because she had so much love and support from her family, she was brave enough to attempt something completely different from anything she had done before.

Hilary was the longed-for daughter after three boys. Her parents were delighted and never was a baby fussed over so much by older brothers, grandparents and so on.

She was a very easy baby and all the love and attention showered on her helped her to grow into a very self-confident little girl. The boys made sure she didn't become too much the dressed-up doll her mother would have liked, by scoffing, as boys will, if she behaved prissily and refusing to let her join in their games. As a result, she was pretty balanced.

Hilary did very well at school and was eventually offered a place at Cambridge. None of her brothers had gone to university. One was a computer whizzkid and had gone straight into a computer company from school. The second had gone into the Metropolitan Police, and the third had set up his own kitchen-fitting business with a friend. They were all amazed at the thought of their little sister going to Cambridge University.

They were even more amazed when she changed her mind and decided that she really wanted to go to art school and enrolled for a year's foundation course. She went on to do a sculpture course at the Camberwell School of Art and finished up at the St Martin's School of Art, teaching in the sculpture department.

Her parents felt they had a little stranger in the family. True, her mother had been quite good at drawing at school, but that was as far as it went. Hilary became a vegetarian and would appear in weird and wonderful flowing clothes. It was all very odd. However, in time the family got used to it and when she married a teacher at the local grammar school, they were surprised as well as relieved.

The baby of the family is often a PS, an afterthought. Most of the time the afterthought is welcomed and the parents, perhaps with a little more time to spare, really enjoy this rather special child. However, sometimes it can be difficult to readjust when it had seemed the world of endless nappies and bottles was behind you at last.

Mary had originally wanted four children, but by the time she had three energetic boys she decided to call it a day. She had married just after she left school and produced the three boys in quick succession. So by the time the youngest had started school, she was still only twenty-six. She found herself an interesting job working in a library and was enjoying her first taste of freedom when she found to her dismay that she was pregnant again, despite having been fitted with a coil. Her doctor assured her that as the device was still in place she would lose the baby, and so she waited for nature to take its course.

Instead the pregnancy continued, until she went into labour two months prematurely. It was a difficult birth and she was very ill afterwards. 'I didn't see Thomas or touch him for thirty-six hours,' she says. Perhaps because he was premature, when they came home from hospital, he screamed non-stop and didn't sleep through the night until he was three. Her other boys had been no trouble and had slept through the night almost immediately. 'He just happened to be totally different from them, but I didn't recognize it. He needed to be cuddled up in my bed.'

The age gap meant that when the others were in their teens and leading their own lives, Thomas was still only ten and needed parental care and attention. 'I remember thinking that if I hadn't had him I would be free to do what I wanted by then. It was then that I decided to send him to boarding school. It all seemed terribly rational, but I know now that he should never have gone – it affected him very badly.'

Thomas is now twenty-three and has just finished a psychology degree. But he has suffered from serious emotional problems and had a near breakdown in his first year at university. 'It's only about three years ago that I realized how much I hadn't wanted him,' Mary says. 'I've had to work through that, to forgive myself for being a bad mother. I love him very much now: we're much closer. He is able to talk to me, something he could never do as a child. But even now I can still feel resentment towards him.'

Her other children, she says, have always got on well with Thomas, despite the age gap. 'They all adored him. Funnily enough, the rest of the family always said he was the favourite. I think I tried to compensate materially for what I didn't feel for him.'

One of Britain's best-known actors was the youngest child in his family. His older brother and sister were very fond of him, but he was often used as a pawn in his parents' domestic disputes.

When Laurence Olivier was born, his parents were in a state of undeclared war. They had met when his father was teaching at a small country school and his mother, a relative of the headmaster, came to visit. Soon after their marriage, they set up their own school. This was one of the mutual ambitions that had drawn them together. The school prospered, but Gerard Olivier, who came from a strict clerical family, decided one day that he had made a mistake in choosing education as a profession. Tom Kieran, Laurence's biographer, says that his wife protested bitterly, but he went ahead and found himself a clerical appointment at St Martin's Church in Dorking. In spite of feeling that she had been betrayed, Agnes Olivier had to settle into the unwelcome role of a clergyman's wife. Not long afterwards she gave birth to a third child, Laurence.

The next blow fell when Laurence was still a baby. His father decided to abandon the now-familiar surroundings of Dorking for the harsh conditions of London's Notting Hill. This was followed a year or so later by a move to Pimlico. These changes completely alienated Agnes. Now war was declared, and she withdrew from Gerard and refused to either share or instil his religious fervour into their children.

Laurence's sister, Sybille, gives the impression that their home was easy-going and filled with laughter until their father came home, when the atmosphere became uncomfortable and tense. Agnes, unable to shield the older two children, Sybille and Richard, from Gerard's influence, concentrated on her 'baby', smothering him with almost neurotic attention and devotion. His brother and sister also adored him, despite their mother's favouritism, partly because he was a very cheerful child and partly because they felt sorry for him. He wasn't allowed to play any sport, because Agnes thought he might be injured, but also because sport was important to Gerard. So he grew up being useless at sport and was branded a sissy by other boys his age. This infuriated his father. So the young Larry was caught in the middle of the hostilities between his parents.

One thing Agnes couldn't forbid was listening to his father preaching, and Larry was fascinated by this. Knowing when to drop the voice, when to bellow, when to wax sentimental: he loved it all and imitated the pulpit orator at home. Agnes encouraged this, and the recital of monologues from Shakespeare. Larry's brother Richard built him a theatre and all three children had great fun acting together.

Then came boarding school. Richard, by then already established at school, was apprehensive. He had qualms about his little brother's ineptitude at games and Larry duly had a difficult time. But his success in school plays helped to compensate for his failure at sport.

While he was away at school, his mother developed a brain tumour and the last time he saw her, she supposedly whispered as he was about to go, 'Darling Larry, no matter what your father says, be an actor. Be a great actor. For me.' When she died, he was utterly desolate, and he has said that for the next three or four years his emotions were completely frozen. He remembered his mother when he was cast as Kate in his school's performance of *The Taming of the Shrew* and she inspired his interpretation. It was a great success. His father was so shaken by the recreation, he had to leave the theatre and forbade Larry ever to act again.

However, Gerard's prospective new wife heard Larry rehearsing some lines in his room and thought he was a natural. Help was sought from an old family friend, Sybil Thorndike, and on leaving school Larry went to the Central School of Speech Training and Dramatic Art on a scholarship.

Thus began the career of one of Britain's greatest actors. His mother had completely spoiled him, but his father had provided a strong antidote, and his siblings had always been very warm and affectionate. He had many friends and eventually three wives – the first, Jill Esmond, an intellectual, the second, Vivien Leigh, a romantic, and the third, Joan Plowright, an earth mother. He won Oscars and many international awards, becoming a legend in his own lifetime.

*

A youngest child who arrives late in many ways resembles an only child. This can make for a powerful combination, blending the friendliness, openness, relaxed attitude of the youngest child with the self-sufficiency and determination of the only child.

This is a story of poverty to power, if not quite rags to riches, in which an apparently ordinary man became prime minister at the age of forty-seven. Wyn Ellis, his biographer, tells all.

John Major was brought up in the Surrey suburb of Worcester Park. His father, who had been an international music-hall and circus star, ran a garden-ornaments business, but he was in his sixties and his health had begun to deteriorate. His mother worked at the local library and his pram was parked, when he was a baby, just inside the door – sometimes all day. 'That is why,' says his brother, Terry Major-Ball, 'he is so bookish.'

John's brother is eleven years older than he is and his sister is two years older than that. He has said, 'I was a mistake,' but his brother claims his mother *had* planned to have another child. In any event, as the youngest in the family, John was fussed over by his mother, and protected and cared for by his brother and sister. This gave him the confidence and openness so often seen in the youngest child. But because of the age gap he also found himself in the position of an only child, and had to learn to play by himself. That made him quite self-sufficient.

His was a very normal boy's life, breeding rabbits and mice to sell with his friend John Brand, attending the local primary school and then Rutlish Grammar School in Wimbledon. His family were very proud that he got to the grammar school, but it put a big strain on the family finances.

Soon after he started at Rutlish, John's father's business fell into difficulties, the bungalow in Worcester Park was sold and the family moved to Brixton. It was much less leafy, the journey to school was more difficult and, to his embarrassment, John had to wear a second-hand blazer. Occasionally, he used to help out at local church fêtes and it was at one of these that he met Marcus Lipton, the Labour MP for Brixton. After they had chatted for a while, Lipton invited the thirteen-year-old to look round the House of Commons. Sitting in the Stranger's Gallery proved to be a life-changing experience. He had to tear himself away from the place to go home.

Three years later, John decided to leave school before taking his O-levels. Both parents were ill and although his brother and sister were working, more income was needed. He did various jobs and then had to give up work to look after his parents full-time. By this stage he had already joined the Young Conservatives. His father died just before his nineteenth birthday, and he started looking for another job, with the youngest child's 'take on anything' attitude. Rejected as a bus conductor because, at six feet, he was too tall, he eventually found work with the District Bank.

There he started taking the Banking Diploma. 'I realized it was a qualification I could get without being articled,' he says, 'that I could get it while working and continuing in politics, and that I could take it in stages.' He used to get up at 5 a.m. and go to bed at midnight to fit in his study, daytime job and evening politics. In 1966 he succeeded in all his exams and applied for a job in Nigeria with the Standard Bank.

After only six months he was back in the UK, having smashed his leg in a car accident. He was away from work for a year, fortunately fully paid, and was able to do much valuable reading. He knew the direction he wanted to take. His father had been a true-blue Tory, and having been brought up in the States was a great believer in the American Dream – that any man prepared to work hard enough can get what he wants. This was no doubt one of the factors in Major's subsequent determination to promote 'a classless society'.

His political career began to take off when he became a Tory councillor in Brixton. Devoting every minute he could to his council work, he soon became chairman of the housing committee, a key position. At this time he met and married Norma Johnson, also a young Tory, and spent several years working very hard in Labour heartlands, waiting patiently for the chance of a parliamentary seat.

In 1976 he was at last adopted and elected MP for Huntingdon, Cambridgeshire, a safe Conservative seat. In his victory speech, he said: 'It's a long way from the back streets of Brixton to the green fields of Huntingdon.' To which came the reply from the audience, 'It may be a long way from the back streets of Brixton to the green fields of Huntingdon, but many of us here tonight have followed that route.'

John and Norma bought a detached four-bedroomed house in Great Stukeley, tucked away behind mature trees. From every window you can see green lawns and flowerbeds. A friend who went with him to look at it heard him say: 'Nobody's going to know what this means to me.' It was an emotional moment.

It was an even longer journey from the back streets of Brixton to Downing Street. Suddenly, Major's political career started an almost vertical climb. He was appointed foreign secretary in 1989, then, only three and a half months later, chancellor of the exchequer, and in 1990 he became Prime Minister.

To what does this youngest/only child owe his success? One of his oldest friends, Robert Atkins MP, has said of him that he's a man who briefs himself up to the eyeballs and has a very good memory. He reads all his papers, and has the ability – essential in a minister – to spot the problem, or spot the political nuance, and act on it. He thinks of himself as a tortoise rather than a hare; someone who moves slowly and carefully from one thing to another. His friends say he is friendly, gracious, generous and unpretentious.

Sir Jimmy Savile comes from a large Catholic family of seven children brought up in Leeds. He is the youngest, or as he describes it, the 'not again' child. Father was a bookie's clerk, though not a 'hustler', according to his family. Sister Joan says that Jimmy was very delicate as a small child, and at one point, when he was five months old, the doctor almost gave him up for dead. But the sixty-nine-year-old, cigar-smoking marathon runner and cyclist has long since laid any fears about his fitness to rest.

The family was very close and well looked after. On the other hand, as Joan says, 'We were taught very clearly right from wrong, and at fourteen we were out on our own. Mum was a great believer in self-help, but if we were in dire straits she would always be there.'

Mum was known as the Duchess, and young Jimmy was thought to be very like her. He had a huge amount of energy, and always liked to get his own way. But the family loved them both. 'He has faith in himself. He listens to advice, but in the end takes his own,' said his sister in an *Independent* feature article.

He makes everything seem so easy. Wherever he goes he has this bounce. He is totally different to the rest of us. We all went to college, but when it came to Jimmy's turn he went to an ordinary Catholic school, because the money had run out. His first job was as a miner and he taught himself French at the same time. Then he had a serious accident. There was an explosion and the roof caved in on his back. We didn't think he'd ever walk again. But then he was up on his bike, plaster from shoulder to hip, leaning flat over the handlebars. That was the end of mining.

'In our family it was the eldest shall be heard; the youngest shall be seen and not heard,' says Jimmy. 'I always used to sit tight until someone decided to pay me a bit of attention. The others were all nice and normal; I was always a bit different. When I was down the pit, I didn't go to the pub with the lads. It wasn't my scene.'

He doesn't have a home as such. Since he's always on the move, he has some seven places around the country where he keeps a bed, a telephone and a microwave oven for warming up soup. He doesn't have friends in the accepted social sense, but he receives about seven hundred Christmas cards every year.

After his mining accident, Jimmy had the idea of taking his wind-up gramophone to entertain people at dances. No one had thought of doing this before. As one of the first independent disc-jockeys, he was offered a job with Radio Luxembourg, followed by a stint with the pirate station Radio Caroline. He was then associated with *Top of the Pops* for several years until the famous *Jim'll Fix It* programme began its eighteen-year run. Through his *JFI* contacts, he became more and more involved in charity work and has since raised millions of pounds for good causes, including £12 million for the National Spinal Injuries Centre at Stoke Mandeville Hospital. And he gives his own time as well as money: at Leeds Infirmary, he talks to the bereaved and helps take bodies to the mortuary.

Like so many youngest children, Jimmy has a great sense of humour. He might command appearance fees of anything up to £10,000, but, he says, as far as his family is concerned, 'it will be, "hey, you," for the rest of my days regardless of whether I'm "sir" three times over.'

Another youngest son who seems to have always been 'a golden boy' is the pop singer Georgios Kyriacos Panayiotou, better known as George Michael. He is not only the youngest child in his family, but also the only son, of a Greek Cypriot father and an English mother.

He describes himself as an optimist and his friends seem to agree that he is easy-going, affable and generous, but not weak. There were no reasons for insecurities to develop in his formative years, spent in a big, rambling house in rural Hertfordshire. Because his father often worked in the evenings, he spent long hours in the company of his mother and two older sisters, a gentle, civilizing influence. And a little boy in a half-Greek family is liable to be privileged and somewhat spoiled. This he admits. 'In comparison with the girls, I was allowed to do as I liked.'

George was born in a flat above a launderette in Finchley in June 1963 at a time when his father was working as a waiter. But the phrase upwardly mobile certainly fits Jack Panos's career. He progressed to a partnership in a restaurant and a semi-detached in Burnt Oak and from there to a beautiful house near Bushey. Kyriacos Panayiotou, or Jack Panos, as he preferred to be known in his adopted country, came from Cyprus with very little money at the time of enosis and the Turkish–Greek Cypriot tensions. He worked hard to provide a good home for his family, explains Tom Parsons, George's biographer.

George loved the new house and big garden. He was a budding naturalist, collecting anything that crawled: beetles, caterpillars, spiders, insects of any kind. He also had a passion for records, which he shared with the boy who was detailed to look after him at his new school, Bushey Meads. Andrew Ridgeley's father was also from the Mediterranean, being half-Egyptian and half-Italian, and Andrew was, at twelve, a slim, good-looking boy. He was the perfect foil for George, and one of the secrets of their close friendship was the way they complemented each other. Andrew had an older brother and was in many ways an archetypal second child – extrovert, popular and very self-confident, but accustomed to having to fight to get his own way, unlike George.

They became inseparable, much to the chagrin of George's parents, who thought that Andrew was a bad influence on George. George had always been a good boy, worked fairly hard at school, been nice to his sisters, but now his grades were slipping. George was to say of him, several years later, 'Andrew totally shaped my life – the whole thing. That's the way I feel about him.'

They started their own band, the Executive, with three friends when they were sixteen. Their first gig was in the Methodist Church Hall in Bushey. The band broke up before long, when the three others left. George and Andrew wrote some songs together, and although Andrew's contribution was never to be as significant as George's, his blind ambition made up for what he lacked in musical vision. He encouraged, prompted, insisted they finished the songs, and thus Wham! was born.

After much hard work and many disappointments, they made *Top of the Pops* when they were nineteen. Soon they had three records in the Top 10. They played the clubs, they went on tour, they made it to number 1 and so they went on for the next four exhausting years, reaping more and more success, but with Andrew playing a smaller and smaller part. By this time George was writing, producing and singing the songs.

It was time to move on, and on 28 June 1986 at Wembley Stadium, before an audience of 72,000, Wham! made their swansong. The parting was sad, but it was friendly; there was no acrimony, no greed, and George and Andrew remained friends.

In his autobiography, George Michael, who has gone on to make solo albums, said he thought what people liked best about Wham! was that 'they could see it was based on something real – our friendship'. He goes on to say: 'I'm an optimist, I try to salvage the good from any situation. I've been given a kind of gift, a strong core that's going to take me through any situation. I never believed that I was going to be anything less than a very successful musician.'

George has had several battles with recording companies over the years, and while these were being waged, he allowed himself a fallow period. Time to enjoy his beautiful house and to walk his dog on Hampstead Heath; a period for making plans. For, as his managers, lawyers, friends and family have observed, 'George always knew what he wanted to do.' Now he is moving to put his plans into action, and doubtless, as in the past, he will do it.

To be the youngest child in a large family is in many ways to enjoy the most favoured of all places. Having already had at least two children, the parents will be relatively relaxed about the youngest's progress and character. Yet they will always feel there is something a bit special about their last-born, just as they do, in a different way, with their first-born. This is particularly true if there is a longish gap between the youngest and the previous child, which is often the case when the youngest is unplanned or an 'afterthought'. In such a position, the 'baby' will enjoy the best of both worlds: some of the benefits of being an only child, plus all the advantages of having siblings around, especially since these too will enjoy giving him attention. No wonder such children often grow up feeling very secure and showing a sunny disposition to the world. They expect to get their own way, and often they do.

A minority may be too spoiled to be prepared to make the necessary effort to get on in life. An even smaller minority may be resented because they were unplanned and have cramped their parents' freedom of movement just when the older children were becoming more independent. But generally speaking, from this happy position they are likely to move only upwards – which they often do, like John Major, with considerable velocity.

5   The Only Child

As children, we are dependent on our parents for survival, but our relationship with our siblings goes to the core of our identities. We carry the history of such relationships out into the world with us. But if there are no brothers and sisters, we have only the parental relationship, which is consequently much stronger. It can be very supportive and encouraging; it can be claustrophobic and alienating; it can promote too much inter-dependence and it can be very demanding.

'I can spot an only child at twenty paces. It's something about the space they always need, the lack of ability to really engage with anyone else or to be able to share themselves,' says a child psychologist who has worked in family therapy for many years.

But is there a typical only child, instantly recognizable to those who know what to look for? Except to those with years of experience, perhaps not; but there are certainly some typical only-child characteristics, which have developed as a result of the child being the focus of parental love and attention – and, of course, expectations, which can impose a heavy burden.

Talk to any only child about these traits and – after his initial surprise that you have found him out – he will acknowledge that he does indeed possess many of them. Indeed, any two only children are more likely to exhibit similar personalities than two siblings from the same family. The characteristics are similar to those of the first-born, but because in the only child they are not modified by dethronement by a second child, as they are in the case of a first-born, they develop in a different way.

There is a social maturity acquired through constant contact with adults, but opposed to that, an emotional immaturity in that only children expect to have everything they want, including their own way. For most, coping alone encourages self-confidence, self-possession and self-sufficiency. As no sibling teasing has been available, they are often not amused by practical jokes and are on the whole fairly serious.

The authors of *Only Child*, Jill Pitkeathley and David Emerson, say their research revealed that only children are distinctively different from all others. The popular image of the spoiled, selfish, self-centred but successful only child is far from the complete picture. There are great gains – of parental love and undivided attention – but also great losses, especially the absence of sharing with other children.

Only children themselves often fail to recognize how much the way they behave in relationships and socially stems from their status. They tend to feel that any odd behaviour is just part of their own identity, since in their formative years they didn't have a brother or sister against whom they could compare it or test reactions. Furthermore, a childhood without siblings leaves a legacy of burdens which present themselves as problems with greater force in adult life than they do in childhood.

At least two authors, P. D. James and Colin Dexter, have made their heroes only children. Both Adam

Dalgleish and Morse are different from the usual bluff, sensible chief inspectors met in detective novels. Both give the impression of being troubled, introverted and highly sensitive.

There are undoubtedly unique pressures and responsibilities for the adult only child, and often all is far from rosy behind the assured and confident exterior usually presented to the world. Talking to several only children revealed different reactions and ways of dealing with this situation.

Davy is among those who really regret having no siblings. He is very much aware of this lacuna in his life and readily acknowledges it.

The only child of a Welsh family, he is very successful, urbane, charming, and has many friends. To all outward appearances, he is very stable and well adjusted. He works as a sales director with a multi-national company, and has inherited the famous Welsh silver tongue. Yet he says that as an only child he always felt very much alone; even now, although he's happily married with two sons, he often feels lonely. 'I would happily take on all the problems of having brothers and sisters to be able to share childhood memories, family memories, with them.'

Davy's father was a Methodist minister who was very strict and had great ambitions for him. His mother was very much in awe of her strongly principled husband, but nevertheless tried to protect her son from the pressures his father put on him. When Davy slipped down the road for a game of snooker with the boys, she always covered for him. His father had not had the opportunity of a university education and was determined that Davy should. '"Study, boy, study," he used to say to me,' Davy recalls. But Davy was more interested in getting out of the oppressive atmosphere of the house as often as he could and having some fun.

Often, however, he couldn't escape, and, like many only children, he had a make-believe sibling.

Sometimes Billy, sometimes Jenny. They were either a big, bossy brother, a young, worshipping sister or a little baby brother, and other variations on the family theme. I also had a fantasy friend called Evan. We read books together, played football together and I can still conjure him up today, although I wouldn't want anyone to know about that.

I have three friends I've known since school and we still meet up and go off together, perhaps to a game of rugby or something like that, and that has meant a lot to me. I suppose I have to admit that I've been the one who has kept the quartet going, keeping in touch and arranging things.

As far as my own family is concerned, I have two sons, and I know I make much more of them than my friends do of their children. They're grown up now, but I see them often and always telephone them. My wife is from a family of four so she doesn't quite see what all the fuss is about. Fortunately she is very understanding, and the boys are also very good in the way they respond. I never get the impression that they're thinking, 'Oh God, it's the old man again, what does he want this time?'

✻

Often only children have older parents, for obvious reasons, and the burden of ageing parents therefore arises earlier in the child's adult life. It can be more difficult for an only child to cut the umbilical cord, particularly if a parent or both parents become dependent on him.

William is the only child of a couple from fairly underprivileged circumstances themselves who did well and raised their living standards and lifestyle considerably. They decided to limit their own family to one child: both had come from large families which, they felt, had overstretched resources. Everything was focused on William. He could do no wrong, but at the same time his parents' expectations were high, both educationally and socially. Fortunately he was very intelligent, and had no difficulty in keeping near the top of his form at exam time. He would be asked about his friends at school and quizzed on their social background. It was almost as though his parents were proving their success through him, vicariously experiencing his achievements.

He was always very self-sufficient and appeared very grown-up for his age. He had friends, but no really close ones, and spent most of his free time with his parents. He learned to play golf with his father, and went away at weekends with them. Even before he reached his teens he was treated as an adult.

William was just about to go to university to study law, to the delight of his parents, who were so proud at the thought that their son would be a lawyer, when his father had a fatal heart attack. His mother was completely shattered, and William dealt with everything, informing family and friends, contacting his father's employers, paying outstanding bills and arranging the funeral. When his mother recovered, a decision had to be made about whether he should still go to university or not. He desperately wanted to go, partly to get away from the sadness of his father's death and his mother's grief, but also to get on with his life.

Inevitably, his mother used a certain amount of emotional blackmail to persuade him to stay and support her. He was faced with a terrible dilemma. Eventually their family doctor suggested a compromise: a dispensation on medical grounds to start a term later. This was obtained, but when the time came for William to leave, his mother had become so dependent on him, emotionally and physically, that he didn't go. Instead he got a job with a local company. He is still there today, living, at the age of fifty-five, with his mother, who now needs constant care.

The self-sufficiency and self-possession of only children can be a great help in coping with the difficulties of their lives. Ann, a teacher in her late thirties, is the only child of older parents. Her life, she says, has been one of inescapable responsibility: her parents have been ill for most of the last fifteen years, and she is constantly worried about one or other of them. As a child she was always in adult company and her father, fifteen years older than her mother, often referred to her as 'my boy', and expected a well-informed, intellectual daughter who could debate issues with him. Her mother was brought up in India and had never got used to the less pampered life at home. She retreated to her bed whenever she could and became a semi-invalid when Ann was still quite young.

Ann went to the local primary school until she was eleven. She was very quiet and, the teachers noted, self-sufficient, yet friendly and helpful in an undemanding way. When she was asked to tea by neighbouring children, she found it a difficult experience. There was so much shouting and banging about from other members of the family and loud music in the background that she felt overwhelmed. She did ask one child back, and things seemed to be going quite well until her father started asking what books the child had read.

Switching to the big comprehensive a couple of miles away proved a great test for her fortitude. At first she found it excruciating, since she was very shy and blushed a lot. She was teased unmercifully for her use of long words and her bookishness. On the other hand, having always been treated as an equal by adults, she had quite strong opinions, and was able to keep her end up in any argument or discussion. After a while she settled down and made a few friends, to the extent where she came to hate the thought of the long summer holidays and felt acutely lonely at home.

Ann doesn't feel bitter or resentful about having to look after her parents now, but she does say how wonderful it would be to have a brother or sister. When she was about fifteen years old, she used to fantasize about having a sister. It is not so much that she wishes to share her responsibilities, she would just like to be able to ring up a brother or sister and talk about the many little everyday problems that seem to crop up more and more frequently.

She looks to the future with some trepidation and wonders how she is going to manage. But, like most only children, she is very close to her parents and wants to help them as much as she can. Since there is no one else, she has no alternative.

Some only children become so self-sufficient and alienated by such demands, or by the hothouse atmosphere, that they cut the umbilical cord and escape.

Janet is a middle-aged writer and the mother of three children. As an only child herself, she feels there are obvious advantages and disadvantages to this status. Because the parents are inexperienced, the first child is expected to be perfect, an expectation that is usually modified when a second arrives. If there are no more children, they don't always realize that, if they can live through the temper tantrums of 'terrible twos', for instance, their son or daughter will eventually end up behaving reasonably, perhaps even going so far as to say please and thank you.

Janet's parents 'had to get married' because her mother was pregnant with her, so she feels the obligation to be perfect was even greater. She felt she was being given an image to live up to, rather than being allowed to be who she wanted to be. As a sensitive child, she found it painful when she was drawn into her parents' relationship. They had frequent arguments and she found herself caught in between them, trying to sympathize with her mother and placate her father, like a miniature adult. She longed for brothers and sisters and kept dropping hints to her parents. But her mother was, she says, a failed feminist, and children and husband were the enemy, a ball and chain.

Janet found school very difficult, particularly as a teenager. She wasn't used to the rough and tumble of life with siblings and her classmates used to play silly jokes on her and make a fool of her. Like many only children, she was very book-orientated and had her own group of imaginary friends, who were much more satisfactory than her real ones.

But on the other hand there were advantages. One of the most important for her was that, as a result of feeling so alone, she made a greater effort to make connections with people outside her family than she might otherwise have done. This was not easy, since she felt emotionally isolated – she was reserved and not at all demonstrative. But she persevered and became accustomed to trying to relate to other people and making her own friends. This stood her in good stead when she became a journalist on a national daily newspaper.

Janet thinks another benefit is that 'your parents can afford to do more for one than for, say, four offspring'. She had a very good schooling, lived in nice houses and travelled a lot with her parents.

Janet's parents are dead now. Bringing up her own children, she says, helped her to finally throw off the only-child feeling. She wanted to be open and to relate directly to them, so introspection and feelings of loneliness seemed inappropriate – and besides, there was no time for them.

Her own three children also seem to follow the classic pattern of birth order. The eldest boy feels a strong sense of responsibility. Since his father died not long ago, he has taken on the role of head of the family more than willingly. The middle child, another son, is still desperately trying to find himself and goes from one crisis to another. He cannot understand how the youngest child, a girl, can be so happy-go-lucky and laid back. Her mother finds her a delight as she sails through life without a care in the world.

The advantages of being an only child can outweigh the difficulties – Ben certainly seems to have no complaints. He is adamant that it has never worried him at all, and that in any case, he has never known anything else. The only son of older parents, with two doting aunts, he admits he was probably 'the original spoiled brat from the moment I was born'. But as a child he was left very much to rely on his own resources and comes across now as an extremely self-sufficient adult.

Ben was born not long before the Second World War, and his childhood home was in Stanmore in Middlesex. His parents kept him with them as long as they could during the bombing, but it eventually became so heavy that he was sent to a kind family in Cornwall with other evacuees from London and the surrounding area. Not yet seven, at first he was terribly homesick and miserable, but this soon passed and his main memory is of days of rural bliss playing on a nearby farm with other children and animals.

When he returned to London, his parents decided that he needed the company of other boys and sent him off to prep and then public school. He was very good at games, particularly cricket; he was always popular, and like many children of older parents, very intelligent, so his years at school passed very comfortably. He read languages at university and discovered he was a natural linguist, eventually acquiring around eight languages. He put his gift to great use when he started to travel worldwide as an executive salesman in the engineering field. Whether in Russia or Brazil, he was able to communicate fluently – or if he wasn't, with typical only-child dedication, he would make sure he soon could.

Travelling constantly was no problem: he enjoyed his own company and made friends and acquaintances in most of the places he visited. Since he was good-looking, undemanding and well informed, he was a welcome guest at any social gathering.

Ben married and had two children. Now grown up, they find him good company, always interested in a slightly detached way, and even his ex-wife (who grew tired of his constant absences, which he refused to reduce) still sees him frequently. He is now semi-retired, but still travels and plays cricket, and is still happy to be an only child.

Sometimes a sibling can become, tragically, an only child through the death of a brother or sister. This can be doubly hard for the surviving child, for not only has she experienced bereavement – sometimes at a very early age – but she then bears, in addition to parental sadness, the full burden of their love, fears, attention and expectations.

This happened to Suzie, who is now thirty, married and enjoying a successful career in publishing. She was sixteen at the time of her older brother's death in a remand home from an epileptic fit. The family was a very traditional middle-class one: the mother was wife and home-maker, the father commuted every day to his job in the City, and the son and heir was sent away to school at the age of seven. Suzie was only four when he left for school, so they never had the opportunity to be close. When he came home for weekends or holidays they would initially be pleased to see each other, but there would be strife after a couple of days because he would want her to play football and she would refuse.

Her parents soon realized that Suzie, in spite of being a girl, was the brighter of the two children. She was in many ways the archetypal eager-to-catch-up, lively, competitive second child. So she was sent off to school too, at about the same time as her brother left prep school for public school.

As Suzie entered her teens, she and her brother became closer, enjoying pop music and parties together. He wasn't doing well at school and wanted to leave after his O-levels, but his parents insisted he must stay. He started to take soft drugs and eventually he was expelled. His father found him a job in the City, which seemed to work for a while. But when Suzie and her parents went on holiday to France, leaving him behind with neighbours, he quarrelled with his hosts on the second day and left home.

For the next few months he wandered about, occasionally turning up at home, and gradually became more and more involved with drugs. Somehow, it seemed terribly inevitable that he would end up in a remand centre, and so he did. He had had several mild epileptic fits earlier in his life, for which the doctors gave him medication, but at the age of nineteen he suffered a major one, and it killed him.

Suzie and her family were devastated. And suddenly she felt the weight of all the responsibilities of an only child on her shoulders. She had to help her parents with their grief and guilt, and to try to make up for her brother's death and lack of success. In addition, her mother wanted her 'to be happy and enjoy life'. Suzie threw herself into work and did indeed succeed, but for years she was almost clinically depressed. She got some help from a counsellor and gradually came to terms with her heavy responsibilities. Getting married helped enormously, and she is expecting a baby soon. Although her parents are delighted, she feels that if she had become pregnant before or just after marriage, they would have been disappointed. It had to be 'right'.

She is aware of the enormous pressure she faces as the only child, but she loves her parents and they her, so she will do her best to cope with it.

Many figures in literature, politics, sport and the theatre are only children. Their characteristic self-confidence and self-sufficiency has doubtless helped some of them to succeed in these very competitive fields. How has their single status affected their lives?

Gayle Hunnicutt is an American actress from Fort Worth, Texas, who first visited England when she was sixteen with her entrepreneurial Aunt Hazel. She has been quoted as saying that Fort Worth bored her silly. The atmosphere was stultifying; the sterile gentility and conventions seemed like a social dusk to her. She felt she could never be part of it. Her parents were not wealthy, which set her apart from most of her peers, many of whom were the children of oil millionaires with their ballgowns and debutantes' dances.

Although her parents doted on her, they didn't ease her loneliness as an only child. They were reclusive people. 'I don't remember them ever going out,' she has recalled. She would return from school to a silent house – often her mother would be lying in bed because 'she wasn't very well'. To this day, Gayle says, she finds the hum and buzz of a busy home – children shouting, the washing machine going – strangely compelling. 'I lived in a bungalow as a child and longed for a real house with stairs.' She now lives in a four-storey terraced house in one of London's more prestigious villages.

Aunt Hazel, a very lively lady, made life bearable. She ran a charm school for debs and took twenty sixteen-year-olds to England every summer as part of their cultural education. One year Gayle joined the party: it was a chance to escape and made her aware of other possibilities in life.

At eighteen she left Texas and got a full scholarship to read English and drama at the University of California and Los Angeles. Her parents refused to give her money to live on. 'They knew if I left I'd never return.' But she had the self-sufficiency of an only child and she knew she would manage somehow. She worked every vacation to pay her way. 'I'd allow myself nine cents a day for a Coke.'

After college, she stayed on in California and got an agent, and finally a contract with Universal Studios. She met her first husband, the English actor David Hemmings, at a Santa Monica party. They married soon afterwards. His career was on a high and she didn't see the dangers. It never occurred to her that he wouldn't or couldn't love her as she loved him. 'What you don't learn as an only child is that not everybody will love you,' she says. 'You're so used to being the focus of attention that you expect it wherever you go. It's frightening when you run into your first brick wall.'

She has now been married to Simon Jenkins, a former *Times* editor, for seventeen years and feels a sense of stability in this country that will keep her here for a long time to come.

Nick Faldo is one of the greatest golfers of the twentieth century and has come to embody the essence of the competitive sportsman. 'I was an only child. I believe that was the single most important factor in the development of the part of my character that has led me to become a champion golfer,' he says in his autobiography.

Nick was the apple of his parents' eye and received total encouragement from them in the pursuit of whatever interest – usually sporting – grabbed him during his formative years. As a child he lived with his parents in a council house in Welwyn Garden City. His father was in the finance department of ICI Plastics, his mother was a cutter and pattern-designer, and although there wasn't much money to spare, and certainly no nights out in expensive restaurants, they always managed to buy him a good cricket bat or a fine fishing rod when he wanted it. His father introduced him to fishing and he still tries to sneak away when 'the river calls'.

Nick Faldo was a fourteen-year-old when he saw Jack Nicklaus on television playing in the 1971 US Masters at Augusta. From that moment he was hooked. Within five years of taking up golf, he had moved from amateur status to become a tournament professional himself. It was his single-minded search for perfection that took him to the top. He has the self-confidence and self-possession that comes from always being the centre of attention, and the self-sufficiency developed from having to amuse himself for hours as a child. He has always been content with his own company, he says. As a result, the solitude of the practice ground and the days spent there building a golf swing were a pleasure to him.

He needs his space and can come across as aloof. Faldo has been described as an enigma who works in a cocoon of concentration, ignoring any disturbance, including anyone wishing him a good morning. Not surprisingly, he has had problems with the media, and even nowadays his attempts at humour often look ham-fisted, as he admits. 'They want me to play like Seve, charm like Arnold and talk like Trevino. Well, I can't – so too bad!' Many people find it hard to warm to him, but there are few on the circuit who do not respect him. For Faldo, that is probably enough.

E. M. Forster, whose six remarkable novels include *A Passage to India* and *Howards End*, wrote his first book when he was twenty-six, but unlike many only children, he was not a self-confident child. His father had died of consumption in 1891 when he was two years old, and becoming the focus of all his mother's anxieties and concerns had an undermining effect on him. Yet he acquired the self-possession and detachment associated with the only child to become a successful and dedicated writer.

In human terms at least, Morgan would have gained greatly from having brothers and sisters with whom to argue and fight. He was a delicate child, and his mother fussed and clucked over him, eventually succeeding in keeping him, more or less willingly, at her side for the rest of her life.

They moved when he was four from central London to Hertfordshire, where Morgan's mother deliberately kept her distance from most of their new neighbours. In addition to the money left by her husband, a wealthy great-aunt had made sure that she and Morgan, and particularly Morgan, would be provided for. His mother was a bit of a snob and deigned to mix with only two of the local families: the stockbroker's and the rector's. This isolation effectively separated Morgan from any potential friends. His mother, 'in her kindness', as she described it, let the garden boy off on Wednesday afternoons to play with him. He was Morgan's only friend, and the afternoon spent with him was 'the happiest time of the whole week', observes his biographer, Nicola Beauman, who goes on to say: 'With a little genuine kindness, genuine thoughtfulness for a lonely child, his life would have been quite different.' Having no one to play with, he became a little adult, like so many only children. There was a grown-up quality about him and a maturity of thought that seemed strange in one so young.

It was only when he moved on from a very conventional and hearty public school to King's College, Cambridge, that he began to feel a little more comfortable. The academic atmosphere was more congenial, individuality was encouraged and there were even a few people who seemed like-minded.

Subsequently, he and his mother moved several times, but he maintained his links with Cambridge. She died when he was sixty-six, and he spent his last twenty-three years at King's as an honorary fellow. It is often said – though the argument is rather facile – that the only son of a possessive and protective mother is prone to develop homosexual feelings. Morgan Forster was reluctant to admit to such feelings, but his novel *Maurice*, which deals with a homosexual relationship, was based on his own experiences.

Enoch Powell provides a classic example of the doted-upon loner. His parents were both schoolteachers with working-class roots and his background was strongly Methodist. Powell himself has written: 'My childhood is very much my mother . . . She was also my first teacher . . . right up to the sixth she took a part in my learning, encouraging me and helping me and very much working with me.' His mother, Ellen, taught herself Greek as a schoolgirl, the better to study the New Testament. Powell's biographer, Patrick Cosgrave, says: 'Ellen Powell found in him the perfect recipient of her own drive and ambition. He loved it all . . .' His father seems to have been a warm presence – 'another boy around the house' – but not a great deal more than that.

Powell was reading encyclopaedias at four and at eight he organized a local children's debating society. This he used as a platform to elaborate on his theory that Bacon and not Shakespeare had written *Henry V* and *A Mid-*

summer Night's Dream. Later he went to King Edward's Grammar School in Birmingham, which then held the record among British schools for the highest Oxbridge entrance levels. He took no part in team games or other group activities, apart from playing the clarinet in the school orchestra. This he enjoyed, but he eventually gave up playing and listening to classical music because, he said, 'I don't like things that interfere with one's heartstrings. It doesn't do to awaken longings that may not be fulfilled.' That fear of emotions and need to stay detached is characteristic of this 'grown-up' type of only child.

No less typically, Powell set his sights on becoming the foremost classical scholar of his time. At Trinity College, Cambridge, to which he won a scholarship, he used to work from 5.30 a.m. to 9.30 p.m. behind locked doors. If anyone tried to interrupt him, he was apt to be extremely rude.

He was rewarded with all available classical prizes, gained the inevitable first and then took up the classics professorship at Sydney University, Australia, aged twenty-five. He was shy with female students, but otherwise deemed to be arrogant and aloof. He seems to have relaxed somewhat in the army during the Second World War, when he became one of the youngest brigadiers and was considered a very good tactician.

Brilliant though his subsequent career in conservative politics was, his obsessional qualities proved his undoing. Had a sibling or two teased him vigorously, he might have acquired greater humanity, and so have avoided being consigned to the political wilderness.

*

The lives of both E. M. Forster and Enoch Powell illustrate the dominant role that parents, and especially mothers, play in the development of only children. The fact that these unique offspring are the focus of their parents' attention and ambitions can prove either wonderfully encouraging or horribly oppressive – or a bit of both. The tightness of these bonds is likely to be felt again in later life, when the only child faces sole responsibility for parents as they decline into old age. Sometimes, such as when father or mother dies young, the burden of being supportive is imposed virtually from childhood.

As we have seen, only children often wish they had the company of siblings. As it is, they are obliged when small to face the hurly-burly of school and the rough behaviour of their contemporaries without any preparation within the family. Being often prematurely bookish and used to the company of adults, they are all the more likely to be teased and bullied. From these experiences they are liable to emerge notably self-sufficient, sometimes to the point – as with Nick Faldo and Enoch Powell – of seeming arrogant and aloof. Spurred on by their parents' ambitions for them, they are at once privileged and vulnerable: this seems a good formula for success, judging by the high number of only children who achieve it.

6   Large Families

Today's normal family is the nuclear family, that is, mother, father and children. This is the immediate family, the intimate family, sometimes called the family of procreation. Then comes the so-called family of orientation – aunts, uncles, cousins, grandmothers and grandfathers – followed by the family of kinship, which ranges a little further afield, and includes second cousins, great-aunts and so on.

The *grossfamilie*, or large extended family, has been disappearing in England for several generations. In the past it was a practical arrangement: the older women of the family were needed to help run the household and look after the children, which in the days before contraception were more numerous than today, and in their turn old people were cared for within the family. Nowadays privacy is treasured, labour-saving gadgets make domestic life easier and people are in any case much more likely not to live close to their parents and other relatives.

So the nuclear family has become the norm – and since the beginning of this century, when parents were first encouraged to have fewer children, and contraception became easier and more effective – a small nuclear family. People expect higher standards of living, education has been extended to all and its quality has risen, and society has become more competitive.

Yet although small families predominate, a substantial number of children still grow up in large families, in which the dynamics are naturally very different.

As in the classroom, the larger the family, the fewer opportunities there are for individual attention and expression. Greater discipline must be exerted and less discussion is possible. The organization, the interaction, the behaviour and the problems involved are all different.

A 1959 survey by US William T. Carter Foundation examined a hundred two-child families and a similar number of families with six or more children. Their findings showed, hardly surprisingly, that the larger the family, the greater the need for good household organization. Jobs must be assigned to the children, which will tend to make them conscientious and reliable. If it does not, they will probably be kept in line by the older siblings.

As large families cost more to run they are more likely to experience economic ups and downs. An income ample to support two or three children is hardly enough for seven or eight. Difficulties grow with weight of numbers in other ways: there will be more food and clothes to buy, more children to break arms and have their appendix out, measles will be spread to many rather than few. Such pressures will take their toll on the parents.

They will be less vulnerable, on the other hand, when it comes to bringing up the children. A mother of seven is likely, crises apart, to be generally more relaxed. She will know from experience that each child develops at his or her own pace and goes through phases, that however unlikely it may seem now, the terrible two-year-old will become an adorable four-year-old. She has learned to exercise judicious neglect.

Children from large families sometimes speak of emotional deprivation, of a parent not having enough time to satisfy all the young ones. But although the parent–child tie may be weakened, caring siblings will largely compensate for this. Indeed, all those brothers and sisters create a sense of security in large families. They form a cohesive group for defence, playing, confiding, teaching – even plotting against the parents. There is emotional security and a measure of mutual economic support.

If, for example, one sibling's funds are low, the 'clan' can help out. In small families, security comes directly from the parents. Large families are like a miniature society: they provide vital social tools, giving brothers and sisters a realistic preparation for dealing with others, particularly of the opposite sex, throughout life.

Apart from a tendency to feel neglected, the only other negative characteristic that emerges is a certain loss of identity from being one of so many. Some children also find it difficult to make friends outside the family.

For any family, the day's big meal is important. That is when the talk is of broad interest, and news is exchanged about who is doing what. It is essential communication time, almost a family forum. Even the younger members have a chance to blossom verbally in what can resemble a personality clinic.

In Victorian times, families of twelve and fifteen children were common; today they are a rarity in the

developed world. There are a few religion-based exceptions: for example in west Finland, where members of
the Laestadius Church, a movement within the main-
stream Finnish Lutheran Church, are forbidden any
kind of contraception. Among its hundred thousand-odd
members, families of fifteen are normal. Some even
reach twenty, necessitating an informal shift system for
meals, an industrial-sized washing machine and a deep-
freeze resembling a small hut.

Anyone from a large family will say that it inevitably
breaks up into pairs or groups; that there is usually one
child who doesn't quite fit in. Often it is someone in the
middle of the family. In this larger setting, the middle-
child syndrome can be all the more devastating, producing an even greater feeling of loneliness.

A Canadian from Quebec, talking about her six
brothers and sisters, recalls that this situation was demonstrated quite clearly in her family. Her father is a
successful solicitor and her late mother had, she says,
been 'just a breeding machine', brought up to believe
that one married to procreate. She was happy enough
with her role in life and proud of her children.

The first group consisted of the eldest boy, who
became a solicitor, the second, a priest, and the eldest
girl, a psychotherapist. The second group contained
three girls, a journalist, a university professor and another
lawyer. The odd one out was the fourth child, Pierre. He
was crazy about sport, a very good skier and ice-hockey
player, and a complete non-intellectual who hated his
book-obsessed family about as much as they hated him.
He was moody and at times violent, and said he didn't

care about the family and didn't want to go to university like the others. 'But all he really wanted,' says his sister, with the benefit of hindsight, 'was to belong and to be loved by the rest of us.'

Pierre's saving grace was his good looks, in which he found refuge and comfort. His sister recalls a photograph of four pretty girls kneeling adoringly at his feet while he grinned happily.

There was a happy ending to this family saga: Pierre met and married a nurse, a very strong girl who thought he was wonderful. She was ambitious for him, and persuaded him to show his family that he could be successful too. He was able to combine medical studies with his enthusiasm for sport so he decided to try to become a doctor. With his young wife's encouragement 'and almost heroic support', his sister says, he finally qualified. 'He is now a very popular and caring doctor in Quebec and we are very proud of him.'

The all-embracing nature of a large family is often singled out as an advantage, but in some cases it can be both claustrophobic and lonely.

Margaret is a thirty-year-old writer who comes from a family of nine children, three girls and six boys, in which she is number seven. She says that when they look back on their childhood, they all say how wonderful it was. But thinking about it more deeply, she realizes that it was by no means all sweetness and light. The family lived in a large, isolated house in the country. There were no other children nearby, so they were thrown into each other's company. At school they found it difficult to form relationships with other people – even now, only two of the nine are married. As in all large families, there were the 'older' ones and the 'little' ones. Margaret was a 'little' one, along with her two younger brothers.

Margaret's father is an artist, a talented painter of whom they are all proud. But, she says, he wasn't at all sensitive when it came to his children. In many ways he was completely unemotional, and appeared to believe that the only way to run a large family was along military lines. It was like being at boarding school, she remembers. They all had to stand by their beds, hair brushed, hands clean and so on, ready for inspection. She was frightened of her father, and her mother seemed a rather remote person, whom she is only just beginning to get to know and like – it was well known, she says, that Mother 'preferred the boys'. Margaret's eldest sister, Jo, was the 'little mother'. 'We went to Jo for everything – money, help with homework, sorting out fights, just everything. Even when I went to hospital, she was there by the bed when I woke up.'

Margaret believes that they did in many ways have a good childhood, but did not receive enough attention individually. 'One of the big ones was sort of assigned to one of the "littles", and Sarah, who was number three, shared a room with me and looked after me,' she says. In some ways it was fun. Sarah was about seven years older and used to come back from the cinema, wake her up and tell her the story of the film – usually a romance – or show her how to use make-up.

Margaret got along best with her two younger brothers. When they left home she shared a flat with one of them for some time. Tom, the brother above her, was the middle child of the family. He was difficult and rather reclusive. The two boys above him were very much a pair, and had a great deal in common. No doubt as a result of this, he was shy and resentful and showed no interest in 'pairing off' with Margaret, which might have been a solution.

The older ones always go back at Christmas, she says, although there are usually rows and someone always has a problem. She doesn't want a large family herself, though she adds quickly that on the other hand she wouldn't want just one child.

She has been writing a novel set in Scotland involving six brothers. She admits she might perhaps be trying to recreate the family. Her greatest wish is to persuade her mother to talk about them all: the basis for another novel, perhaps.

The Bensons are a third-generation north-country family living near Preston in Lancashire. Father is a successful bank manager and mother was a schoolteacher until number five of their six children came along.

The eldest son is named Henry, or Harry, after his father and grandfather, and the second is Charles, after his maternal grandfather. Being the eldest son matters in this family, and much is made of Harry's prowess at school, both academic and sporting. Charlie accepts this, but since he is quick and bright he poses a constant threat to the slower-witted Harry.

Then comes Steve, the clown who is always fooling around. He was a lovely, cheerful baby and enjoyed being the youngest for a couple of years until the longed-for girl, Sheila, arrived. She was much celebrated and totally eclipsed poor Steve. Then, in fairly rapid succession, came two more boys, John and Kim, who soon became the 'little ones'.

The two older boys, Harry and Charlie, were quite good friends, but always subconsciously competing with one another, Harry to reinforce his first-born status and Charlie to challenge it. In a large family it is difficult for a child to accept the sibling immediately succeeding him, and therefore the strongest bond will often be with another brother or sister. So Harry and Steve did things together, and Charlie and Sheila used to get on very well in a teasing way, ganging up on the other two whenever they could. The two 'little ones' used to do things together too, even if it was only fighting.

When Harry went off to 'big school', he arrived home late because of sport and then had to do his homework, and Steve became the odd one out. He tried to attach himself to the other two, but they were not interested.

He was on his own. True, he had a group of friends outside the family, but they were considered a bad influence, and as he got older he spent more and more time with them at beer-drinking video parties. His schoolwork suffered accordingly. When this was noticed at home, his parents decided to move him to another school, and that proved to be his salvation. It had a very good drama group and as Steve had always been a natural actor, he fitted in very quickly.

The drama coach had a lot of TV contacts, and Steve was soon travelling to Manchester at weekends, doing bit parts for Granada TV. So instead of being the family's odd one out, he became the family celebrity, thanks to frequent appearances on TV. His parents were proud of him, his older brothers changed their attitude, Sheila paraded him round her friends and the 'little ones' regarded him with awe.

One of the most famous large families in the world, the Kennedy clan, is in many ways archetypal. The tribal element is strong, and family members share a powerful instinct to close ranks as the enemy approaches. And as in other large families, different alliances evolved with one or even two members being left out.

Inevitably in a family so dominated by the father, the boys played a more significant part than the girls. Young Joe, Jack, Bobby and Teddy were each to show the characteristics of their birth order.

Joe senior was an outstandingly successful Irish Catholic businessman who engineered for himself the post of US ambassador to Great Britain. His relentless emphasis on success had its effect on all his children, but it gave them a reassuring background of great financial security. Having provided more than adequately for the family, Kennedy felt at liberty to indulge himself outside it, and was a well-known womanizer. All of his sons followed this aspect of their first role model to some degree. Young Joe, the eldest son, was tall, handsome and powerfully built. In *The Kennedys*, Peter Collier and David Horowitz report that he had his father's flashing smile, and like his father, he liked showgirls.

He took on the mantle of Joe senior's ambition and was willing to act as his father's lightning rod. He was quite fearless, with an obsessive need to justify himself. Legend has it that in St Moritz he jumped into a bobsleigh for the first time on a run where experienced bobsleighers had lost their lives and came near to the world's record time.

Young Joe was fanatically devoted to the family. He was very affectionate towards his younger siblings. Teddy, the youngest, would come running up when he arrived home and Young Joe would give him a hug as he hoisted him up on to his shoulders.

Although Jack was not 100 per cent fit, he had with his father's help followed Young Joe into the US Navy and been sent off to the 'real' war in the South Pacific against Japanese shipping, while his older brother was stuck in Puerto Rico. Jack took his command role far less seriously than his brother. When his PT boat was sliced in half by a Japanese destroyer, he and his crew were rescued after seven days on a Pacific island and he returned home a hero. At a family party, Young Joe had to drink a toast to his brother, the war hero. A friend sharing his room said he heard him wake in the night and swear to himself that he would 'show them'. The pressures on this first-born were clearly intense.

Joe was about to end his commission when a call went out for experienced pilots for a top-secret mission. Young Joe jumped at the chance to reassert his supremacy over Jack. Checking his plane, technicians found a problem, but he waved them away. He was killed minutes later when the plane exploded.

Jack Kennedy, the second-born, suffered as a child from a wasting disease. Frail and sickly, he was also born with a weak back, but no Kennedy ever whined, so it was stiff upper lip and pain endured silently. He had two things on his mind: his health and his brother. 'Joe plays football better, dances better and gets better grades,' he is quoted as having said. Young Joe overshadowed him in everything.

But although Jack was smaller, he was resourceful, always a threat. He used the skills of the weak: speed and cunning, say Collier and Horowitz.

Young Joe's death hit them all hard, but perhaps his father the hardest. Jack had come to enjoy the competition with his brother and the role of underdog – when not much is expected of you, any achievement is all the more dramatic. His brother's mantle was now his. 'I can feel Pappy's eyes on the back of my neck,' he told a friend. But he rose to the occasion.

His second-born's flamboyance and rebelliousness were channelled into a gruelling campaign to be elected for Congress, during which he was in constant pain from his back. Later, when the young, cynical, death-obsessed Democratic congressman became a presidential contender, the whole family set to work in his support. And so he became the 'new frontier' president, a leader for the new generation: still flamboyant and rebellious, still a risk-taker; but as the most powerful man in the world, obliged to be more responsible in every sense.

That fateful day which everyone of a certain age can remember, he went down to Dallas to do some fence-repairing with Vice-President Lyndon Johnson's supporters. He had been warned of anti-administration feeling, but went anyway, and met his assassin's bullet.

Four girls came after Jack in the family. Rosemary was retarded; Kathleen, in the wake of her father's ambassadorial stay in London, married a titled Englishman; Eunice was religious; and Pat, attractive and vivacious, married the film actor Peter Lawford.

Next came Bobby, the runt of the litter, in the middle of this large family, then Jean and Teddy, the baby. Recognized by all as the odd man out, Bobby was small, unco-ordinated, inarticulate, and his mother worried that he would grow up 'puny and girlish'. And yet this apparently least relevant member of the family emerged as a linchpin. His father saw his potential and reckoned presciently that Bobby 'will keep the Kennedys together in the future'.

Bobby, said to be the most intense member of the family, was brooding, passionate and more Irish than the others. Where Jack sought to avoid responsibility, he embraced it, and loyalty was in his nature. He was the key figure in the Kennedy administration and brother Jack often had occasion to say to his advisers, 'Thank God for Bobby,' when his sibling worked out another strategem to deal with a tricky situation or person.

When Jack was assassinated, Bobby was the rock to which the family clung. He consoled everybody and kept them active. He was inconsolable himself, however, and confided in a friend the pain and agony he was suffering. The guilt of the survivor was no doubt a contributory factor.

Bobby proved to be a good husband, a loving and demonstrative father, son and uncle, and his sister-in-law Jackie received enormous support from him. When he himself became the Democratic senator for New York, he and brother Teddy, who had already served a term, were sworn in together.

A couple of years later, in 1967, Bobby was put under increased pressure to stand as presidential candidate. After some vacillation, he decided to run. Polls suggested that he would win, but it was generally felt that his campaign organization in no way matched the well-oiled machine he had put together for his brother in 1960. Teddy did his best to help. Bobby won the critical Indiana primary and finally California's. After seeing the results come in at his hotel, he went downstairs to make a press statement, cutting through the kitchen to save time. There he was shot. Five minutes earlier he had told his old Harvard friend Ken O'Donnell: 'You know, Ken, finally I feel that I'm out from under the shadow of my brother. Now at least I feel that I've made it on my own.'

Three brothers were now dead. Teddy's initial response was withdrawal. The youngest Kennedy retreated to his boat and disappeared for days, beyond obligation and responsibility. Jean, who came after Bobby and was close to him, could not help. Teddy was the kid brother who cheated in exams, but had an instinctive warmth. He was 'Smilin' Ed', who trailed his brothers and sisters in every way, the afterthought in the family. Yet as his father grew older and more infirm, if Teddy bounced into the room, his face lit up.

He realized, as one of his nephews, Chris Lawford, put it, that 'he couldn't fill Uncle Bobby's shoes, and he didn't try'. On the other hand, he was aware of the importance of his new place in the family. 'I can't let go. If I let go, Ethel [Bobby's wife] will let go, Mother and my sisters will let go. I just can't.'

As the spoiled youngest son, Teddy had long enjoyed drinking and partying: another of his nicknames was 'Cadillac Ed'. But now he drank for a different reason: he was under terrible stress. 'They're going to shoot my ass off the way they shot Bobby,' he told people frequently.

The Kennedys found a safe job for him as Senate Majority Whip. He was still, however – as his friends feared – an accident waiting to happen. It did – at Chappaquiddick, where he drove a young woman over a bridge in his car, crashed into the water and did not report her death for several hours. It was seen as an example of Kennedy recklessness and arrogance.

Teddy's reputation never fully recovered. But although he will never live up to his brothers, he is now admired for his hard work and doggedness.

The story of the Kennedy clan, part of American political history, shows in sharp relief most of the typical advantages and disadvantages of a large family.

In the Royal Shakespeare Company, most of the drama, fortunately, takes place on the stage rather than in real life. One of its younger stars, Stella Gonet, comes from a family substantially larger than the Kennedy clan. She is the seventh of twelve children.

Stella joined the RSC in 1986 for Arthur Miller's *The Archbishop's Ceiling*, in which, as she told a magazine interviewer, 'I only had eight words, but I was onstage the whole time and had to dance and do all sorts of things. Miller came and we all fell madly in love with him. "She's perfect," he said of me, which wasn't hard as I had almost no lines. But that became my nickname in the company, Little Miss Perfect.'

Stella has played many Shakespearean heroines, among them Isabella in *Measure for Measure* and Titania in *A Midsummer Night's Dream*, as well as a leading role in the television series *The House of Elliott*. Her acting career has been conducted mainly within the framework of the two big national institutions, the National Theatre and the RSC. She attributes this to her background, preferring 'situations where families can be recreated'.

Her parents met when her father, a Polish soldier, was stationed at Greenock during the Second World War. They married and moved to Buenos Aires, where their two eldest sons were born. They then returned to Scotland and had ten more children over the next two decades. Mrs Gonet was known locally as 'a great manager' – a very high compliment from the Scots. There was always good, interesting food on the table. Stella's father brought home fresh fish from local rivers and vegetables from his allotment, but his speciality was a rib-sticking soup. He would boil endless carcasses for stock and, breathing in the steam, explain, 'You see, from the death comes life.'

'I was the middle one of a huge brood. That's why I became an actor – it was the only way to get attention. At last I could stand up and speak, and everybody would have to listen to me and keep quiet while I did it,' says Stella triumphantly.

When Stella was twelve, her mother decided to fulfil a long-held dream and go to university. She gathered all six girls around her and asked, 'if we would help take on the duties of the house', says Gonet. So she was shopping and cooking for fourteen of them before she was into her teens. She still finds it difficult to cook for small numbers. Their mother eventually became an English teacher and they are all wonderfully proud of her.

At first Gonet wanted to be a runner. 'Dad was delighted because he was very keen on anything physical. He wanted all his sons to be footballers, and Mum wanted them to be priests. But he was just as happy when I gave it all up to do acting,' she recalls. 'We were all completely besotted by this wonderful man, even if we were embarrassed by the way he would insist on embracing his friends, our friends and even people he didn't know.'

At drama school in Glasgow, Gonet threw herself into 'all the things I should have done when I was fourteen. With five younger than me, I always had to take the wee ones with me wherever I went, so going out with boys and things like that had been out of the question.' Later she added: 'I'm sure that if I got on a psychiatrist's couch, there'd be a part of me that wishes I was an only child, but we're a close family: we all get on together. If anyone needs anything, it's a great network.'

Now thirty-four, Stella Gonet is keen to have a family of her own, but she doesn't want a large one. She is quite clear that 'two or three, not twelve', would be enough.

Another well-known large family, this time Anglo-Irish, have thrived in their academic, political and finally literary spheres. Frank Pakenham, Lord Longford, has been a controversial but well-loved figure for many years. Denis Healey, a fellow socialist, said of him: 'Frank always overdoes it. You can forgive Myra Hindley without making out that she is Mother Theresa.' The columnist Bernard Levin commented: 'Everybody asks the wrong question about Lord Longford, viz., is he barmy? The question is not worth asking: of course he is barmy. What we should be discussing is something quite different: is he right?' His friend, the former *Observer* editor David Astor, remarked: 'It is so easy to treat Frank with the modesty and self-mockery with which he always talks about himself. Really he is a person of great intelligence and of great moral strength.'

Frank Pakenham was a politician for many years, a great friend of Hugh Gaitskell's and leader of the House of Lords in the Wilson era. As the second son in a family of six, it was not he but his brother Edward who inherited the family title of Earl of Longford. But he was offered a peerage by Attlee and became a 'lord-in-waiting' in 1945, inheriting the family title when his brother died in 1961. In addition to Edward there were two sisters, then a gap of five years and two younger children. This led to the family being split into 'Us Four' and the 'Babies', as Peter Stanford recounts in his biography.

Pakenham was introduced to his wife, Elizabeth, by Gaitskell at Oxford. They didn't marry for three years or so and then produced a family of eight children: Antonia, Thomas, Judith, Patrick, Rachel, Michael, Catherine and Kevin. Frank Pakenham was well-meaning, but not very good at fatherhood. After attending Antonia's birth he said he never again wanted to watch a baby being born; nor was he remotely interested in changing nappies. Elizabeth Pakenham, by contrast, loved having babies: she said she suffered from 'the baby itch'. As the family evolved, its identity shifted from the academic to the political and then to the literary: at one point more than twenty years ago, seven of its members had produced twenty books between them, and the flood of words has not been staunched since.

Although they were not poor, there was a puritan streak in the family which caused Michael to joke that he would write a book called Look Back in Hunger. The children grew up in a protected, inward-looking environment, relying a great deal on each other for company, whether in London, Oxford, Sussex or Tully Nally, the family seat in Ireland.

While a small private day school was deemed adequate for the girls, the Longford boys attended Ampleforth, the smart and expensive Catholic boarding school. The eldest son, Thomas, explained that their father was a very ambitious man, very keen on success and wholly unsnobbish: it wouldn't matter whether someone came first in tiddlywinks or the translation of Greek verse – the great thing was to succeed.

Both Antonia and Thomas managed to do so, both at school and university, which made the younger children realize that academic success pleased their parents. Rachel, the third daughter, recalls, 'I wasn't half as academic as my brothers and sisters. Although I didn't particularly rebel against it, looking back, I think my interests, which were more towards the arts, were quite different from those of the others. Nobody said I was inadequate, but I did remember feeling it when my younger brother Michael used to do his exams at the same time as me and get better results.'

When Judith followed Antonia to Oxford, she joined the university Labour club. 'I was proud of being a socialist, but found I wasn't a real socialist,' she explained. She said she felt almost schizophrenic as everyone else seemed to have northern accents and talked about practical everyday issues. It was only then that she realized how upper-middle class the family really was, with their two houses and comfortable lives.

An insight of the relative merits of his brothers and sisters (before Kevin was born) was written by Paddy, aged nine, and appeared in his mother's book *The Pebbled Shore.*

Antonia is a girl, rather clever when laden with responsibility. Mostly she is very nice.

Thomas is a boy keen on photography and bird-watching. On the whole very agreeable and generous.

Judith loves her dolls and treasures them. She adores Antonia. Antonia lets her play with her own exquisite dolls.

Rachel also likes dolls, makes dresses in wool and cotton, being skilled in the art of needlework. She is Thomas's pet – he calls her his 'chubby lassie'.

Catherine is a very jolly and stout young lady.

Michael is the one I like best, and we are both devoted to each other. We both like playing soldiers. I usually let him win a few battles so he is not discouraged. He likes everybody and everybody likes him, but he likes *me* best.

Paddy was a second son, like his father, and Frank Pakenham identified with him strongly, protecting him when, as frequently happened, he was in trouble. Paddy became a successful criminal barrister, but following a sailing accident in which two of his friends drowned, he had a series of mental breakdowns and has given up his practice.

Another tragedy for the Pakenham parents was the

127

death of their daughter Catherine in a car accident. She, like Antonia, had worked for the publisher George Weidenfeld, and had done well as a journalist with the *Daily Telegraph*. She was with two friends driving at night when a lorry hit them. All three were killed instantly.

The centre and anchor of the family was always Elizabeth Longford. She steadfastly supported her husband while retaining her own identity. Even more ardent a socialist than Frank, she had great reservations about him entering the House of Lords, which she had fought to have abolished, but loyalty won the day.

Being part of a large family, then, can be both a daunting and a very supportive experience: daunting, because the children in the middle have to fight for parental attention and may suffer some loss of identity; supportive, because, whatever happens in life, they will always have the clan, with all its loyalties and contacts, behind them. Although children from big families have invariably had most of their rough edges knocked off them within the family, they may be so used to each other's company that they find it difficult to make relationships outside the family, since a large family is in many ways a self-sufficient microcosm of society. Another reaction may be to seek employment, as Stella Gonet did, within an environment that recreates the same atmosphere.

On the darker side, the law of averages dictates that more large families will suffer tragedies than small families – witness the Pakenhams as well as the Kennedys. Much, if not all, human life is there, for worse as well as for better.

7   Twins

Twins have a special place in the family – particularly
identical twins, who are, biologically, two halves of one
person (or two halves of one egg). Seventy per cent of
the fertilized eggs resulting in twins split after early
development has already taken place, and the two
embryos remain in the same membrane. It is now
generally believed that any difference within an identical
pair must be due to non-genetic causes. While identical
twins are inevitably of the same sex, so-called fraternal
twins – the products of two eggs fertilized at the same
time, rather than of one fertilized egg which later splits
– can be of the same sex, or of opposite sexes. Geneti-
cally, they are no different from ordinary siblings, but
are carried in the womb together and born at the same
time. So the differences between them can be due to
either genetic or environmental factors, as with other
siblings.

The bonding or closeness of identical twins cannot be
over-emphasized. It is common for them to have a
private language as young children, for one to feel pain
when his twin is hurt, for them to have telepathic
communication and to show extreme distress at any
separation. Many clinical studies report that one twin is
usually dominant over the other or, more commonly,
acts as a spokesperson. The pattern of dominance can

be quite strong, even in adulthood. The spokesperson is usually the older twin, who also tends to be slightly heavier and healthier. It is estimated that one in six multiple pregnancies ends in the death of one or both twins. The younger twin is often over-protected and shows a marked dependency on the mother or co-twin. According to Mittler, no compelling explanation has been advanced to account for the slight inferiority of twins, as a group, in intellectual functioning and educational skills throughout childhood. But it has been commented upon in many schools and colleges. The gestation period for twins is shorter, on average by three weeks, and the birth weight is in the region of two pounds lower – the average weight of a twin at birth is under 5.5 lb. Fifty-five per cent of twins are born prematurely. Koch reports that they are also, again as a group, below national norms in height and weight and quotes a study in which 873 conscripted Swedish male twins still showed some retardation at eighteen years old, and were found to be below the norm in height.

The arrival of twins can have a strange effect on parents, and bringing them up calls for special 'coping styles'. A Canadian survey of forty-six sets of identical twins, published in 1978, showed that parents speak much less to twins than they do to other children. They also show less affection towards them, hugging and kissing them less often than they do their other children. A single child makes a one-to-one attachment to his mother and to other children, but twins already have an attachment to each other, so any family relationship is immediately a threesome. It's therefore very hard for a mother to bond in a clear way with twins, because they have a connection in which she has no part. When there are other children in the family, twins are likely to be left alone a lot to amuse each other. Such behaviour naturally strengthens the bond between them; moreover, it may well drive the twins in upon themselves, forcing them to seek from each other the stimulation and comfort denied to them by their mother. Several studies report that twins tend to clamour for their mother's attention far more than other children.

Mothers often treat twins as a single unit, for the very practical reason that two children are more of a handful than one. Both will be put to bed, even if only one is tired. Both will be fed solids, though only one may have teeth. Mothers tend to dress their identical twins alike, partly because it's cheaper, and partly because it avoids the charge of favouritism.

If preference is given by a parent to either twin, it can prove particularly painful because such favouritism denies the existence of what they hold most dear: 'oneness'. The effect will be felt throughout their lives.

Twins are generally popular at school, if only for their novelty value. But they are always chosen for team games in pairs. Surprisingly, perhaps, the closeness of twins does not appear to interfere in their relationships with adults outside the family or friendships with other children. But nevertheless they are less gregarious and, predictably perhaps, tend not to have best friends in the way that single children do.

The Twin and Multiple Births Association is flourishing (there are 220 affiliated clubs). They make a conscious effort to emphasize the importance of treating each twin as a separate person, looking for the differences between them rather than the similarities. Books on childcare in many countries have for years recommended this approach.

The private language that twins frequently develop, often because their parents are too exhausted to talk to them enough, is usually their own mixture of new words and pidgin. It sounds like gibberish and acts as a protection against outsiders, but it can hold back their development. When they are separated, for example placed in different classes at school, they rapidly learn to speak properly and communicate with others. As twins grow up into their separate identities, they often deliberately seek different interests and, later, different occupations to escape from the constraints of their relationship and of the way they are perceived by others. This can only be seen as a healthy development.

If separation is left too long, it can be extremely painful. An identical twin, the younger of the two, recounted how she and her sister – who had done everything together, had hardly any friends and didn't feel they needed them, at primary or secondary school – had decided to go to different teacher-training colleges. She said she had had no idea how terrifying it would be. 'I felt completely cut in half. I couldn't focus on anything. I tried to cover up for a few days, but ended up just collapsing one evening. I thought I was dying. What should have been like a new birth felt like death.' With help, she survived, but wishes she had been more prepared for such a traumatic experience.

In 1980, Professor Tom Bouchard of the University of Minnesota conducted what became a famous study, bringing together twins who had been separated for many years for a week's intensive testing. Their medical histories were checked and they had physical and psychological examinations. Although lifestyles varied enormously, the similarities which emerged in many of them were striking. For example, the same illness was found to have occurred at the same stage of their lives; female twins appeared in almost identical outfits and wearing identical jewellery on the same arm; others had suffered similar marital problems to their twins.

For thousands of years twins have been venerated in most societies, often regarded as the agents of miracles in mythology and religion. More negative traditions are to be found, however, in Australasia, Japan and India, where the mother of twins was ostracized and regarded as impure. The Hottentots were so frightened of the possibility of a further twin birth that they removed one of the father's testicles in a misguided attempt to prevent such an eventuality. There are also reports of second-born twins being killed because they were believed not to be 'real' people.

In literature, most of the earlier stories featuring twins make liberal use of the obvious device of mistaken identity, for example, Shakespeare's *Twelfth Night*. As it happened, Shakespeare was himself the father of twins. But in 1848, George Sand's novel *La Petite Fadette* anticipated later thinking by introducing a character who allays contemporary fears of too close a relationship between twins by advising the parents to treat them as two individuals, stressing differences rather than similarities.

＊

Anne and Carol, who are in their early thirties, are typical of many identical twins in that the elder twin usually takes the lead. Anne certainly gives the impression that she is the dominant twin. She sounds quite protective when talking about Carol, but at the same time a little patronizing. Anne works for a publisher. She is married to a businessman and has a baby of fourteen months. Carol was a teacher, but with three children under five, she has given up work and finds life much more fulfilling now than she did when she was involved in her career. She is married to a GP.

They have a brother ten years older and a sister eight years their senior, so they felt almost a different generation. Like most twins, they had their own little world, but in their case it was exaggerated by the age gap between them and their siblings. When they were small, Anne said they more or less entertained themselves. They didn't have a secret language, but Anne thought they were probably slower than the average child to learn to talk, as their mother had difficulty focusing on both of them. They enjoyed yet at the same time disliked being twins. They loved playing tricks on people at school, but they hated the way they were stared at as if they were freaks.

Once they started to grow up, they insisted on wearing different clothes. When they went to university, they chose different towns: Anne went to Oxford and Carol to Reading. By then they were both fed up with being twins, and they didn't experience the misery suffered by some twins when they are separated. Anne says she didn't really miss Carol desperately; she didn't even miss her when she went to Australia for a year. Yet she

134

definitely feels they are two halves of a whole. They have similarities and differences, but these are complementary: together they make a rounded person.

Their mother was fairly conventional, but they were allowed to go more or less their own way: their older sister, Lucy, had forged the path for them, and there was little pressure from their parents involved in their development.

Nowadays they talk to each other about once a week, and are fairly close, especially when a problem or crisis arises. Carol was supportive when Anne was pregnant, and distressed when Anne and her previous partner split up several years ago.

It is Anne, however, who seems to dictate the way the relationship is conducted. And although her sister constantly tries to persuade her, particularly since she had her baby, to give up work, Anne has no intention of giving up her career. One senses that she has always been the more ambitious of the two.

Ollie and Tom are identical twins born within ten minutes of each other. Their father, Frederick, is from an aristocratic east European family: he has a title, a great regard for old values and traditions, and believes in primogeniture. So when he introduces his sons, he always says, 'This is Ollie, my eldest son; this is Tom, my middle son, and Adam is the youngest.'

Frederick went to university in this country to read agriculture, and there met the twins' mother, a horticulture student. They married and went to live on a farm in Shropshire, where their sons were born. Ollie and Tom did not speak properly until they were nearly four years old. They had their own private language and could communicate with one another using the smallest signs and body language, some of which were not even visible to other people. Even now, aged fifty, they know immediately if anything of importance has happened to the other and phoning to confirm or hear the details is merely a formality.

They were sent away to school together and then Ollie went to St Martin's School of Art and Tom to the Portsmouth School of Art, a separation which they both found extremely difficult. They describe it as being in a state of awareness all the time that 'someone' wasn't there. It was more than just missing another person – it was a physical sense of loss as well. But it was only for a year, after which they were both accepted by the Royal College of Art. Tom is now a successful designer and Ollie an even more successful film-maker. They are still very close, yet there is a feeling of rivalry. Although their facial features are exactly the same, physically they seem to complement each other: Tom is concave, Ollie convex. Tom has a slight stoop and a faint aura of rebelliousness, or perhaps resentment; Ollie seems bodily larger, more upbeat and very much in control.

The dominance of the first-born twin is seen in fraternal twins as well as identical ones. Catherine and Susannah are non-identical twins, who nonetheless look like the proverbial two peas in a pod. They were brought up in the Lake District with two older brothers. Their father is a musician and, according to the twins, a confident, rather sexist man. Their mother, who had four children under the age of five, had a difficult job bringing them up, and he gave her very little support.

Their eldest brother was also musical, but reluctant to compete with his father. He therefore channelled his love of music into making instruments, mainly violins. He adored his little sisters and made a great fuss of them, to the annoyance of the second-born son, who was known in the family as the 'monster'. He was incredibly energetic and constantly demanded attention. Discontented and complaining, he made everyone suffer for his dissatisfaction with life. He eventually became so unpleasant that the eldest boy left home at sixteen and moved to London to escape him. Then the second son was left to rule the roost, which suited him and therefore improved matters somewhat.

The twins got on well together as children, but when they took their Eleven Plus exam, Susannah passed and Catherine did not. They bawled their heads off and refused to be separated, but their father insisted. Even at eight years old, Catherine had been a great help to her mother and could be relied upon to carry out any chores she was given, so no one was surprised when she went to work in the local bar and was soon asked to run the restaurant as well. Her sister did well at school and went on to university, thus becoming the family 'intellectual', a status her second brother resented enormously. He hated feeling inferior to anyone, particularly his spoiled (in his eyes) baby sister.

Ten years later, the tensions in the family have almost disappeared. Their father has mellowed and spends more time with his long-suffering wife. The eldest boy has become a Buddhist and is still happily making violins. The second son, after some counselling and training, became the sales manager of a chain of outdoor shops covering the north of England, and his enormous energy has undoubtedly been a great asset there. He works on a commission basis, and is happy now that he is earning far more than anyone else in the family.

Catherine is married and she and her husband run their own three-star hotel not far from the family home. Susannah, the younger twin and baby of the family, works for a publisher in London and looks forward to the weekends she spends with her sister.

There seems to be a love-hate element in many twins' relationships. Angela and Laura have gone through many ups and downs, and although they get on very well now, they tend to see each other for fairly short periods at a time.

Angela, who is three minutes older than her identical twin, refers to her sister quite frequently as the 'after-birth'. They both have red hair and pale skins, but true to form, Angela is the dominant one. She is thought to take after their rather wild, outgoing Irish mother while Laura is more like her more sober and quiet English father. In photographs showing them at eleven or twelve, you look from one to another trying to spot the difference – and it is impossible. 'We had to dress exactly the same and we used to hate it,' says Laura. The nuns at their convent school made them wear badges bearing the initials A and L, but of course they just swapped them around. They were known as the Terrible Baker Twins, and when their parents divorced, and they went to live with their father in Essex, the nuns were probably mightily relieved.

The divorce was not easy, and one of the twins was required to give evidence in court, a painful experience. No doubt the noisy twin, who shouted loudest and longest, was not thought suitable; in any event 'I was the one who had to do it,' says Laura, still with a trace of bitterness.

In Essex they went to a comprehensive school near Harlow where they found they were invariably treated as one person, one unit called the 'twins'. But as they moved up through the school, Angela became head girl and Laura went to France to be an au pair for eighteen months. From then on their paths diverged. Laura decided to go to Athens to teach English, while Angela became the Harlow theatre's stage manager and then joined *Time Out*, where she worked for eleven years. Both girls married, and both husbands were astonished when they first met their respective wives' twin. Angela's Canadian husband said he thought it was freaky how even their mannerisms were the same. Even as adults, they feel they have their own special wavelength. For example, when Laura had a miscarriage, Angela said she sensed something was wrong and got in touch straight away.

After much travelling, Angela settled in Crete, where she has been running a beach restaurant for five or six years. Laura lives in north London and has a partnership in a book-binding company. They feel they are closer now than they have been for several years and see each other quite often, despite the distance. Laura's comment probably sums up their relationship: 'You never need a best friend if you are a twin.'

*

There have been numerous well-known sets of twins: the Barclay twins have risen from being painters and decorators to the new owners of the Ritz Hotel; the Blakeney twins appeared in the soap opera *Neighbours* not long ago; the singing Beverly Sisters of the fifties included a set of identical twins. The underworld produced the identical Kray brothers, who claimed to be in touch mentally, emotionally and spiritually when they were in prison, even though they were physically separated.

There have been several pairs of twins in the sporting field, but most famous among them are surely the Bedser twins.

In his autobiography, the great England bowler Alec Bedser writes: 'We had the often silent conspiracy of twins ... There was never any doubt in the minds of my twin brother Eric and me that we would be cricketers.' They also excelled at football and played for Woking Boys and Surrey Boys.

The Bedsers were brought up in Woodham, Surrey, where their father was a bricklayer employed on a casual basis. If it was too wet to lay bricks, he got no pay. The twins were taken to see their first Test match by the local vicar, a cricket enthusiast.

At school they dressed the same, used many of the same phrases in their essays, and made the same mistakes in maths. The teachers thought they were colluding and moved them to opposite sides of the class, but the similarities continued. When they were fourteen, they both entered a solicitor's office in Lincoln's Inn Fields to train as solicitor's clerks. But they had had enough by the time they were seventeen and chucked it in to join a cricket school in Woking.

Both were natural medium-fast bowlers with a similar run-up. But they reckoned they would have a better chance of being able to join the same county side if they developed different styles and paces, since each team needs a balance of various types of bowlers. They tossed a coin to decide who should be the one to change to off-breaks, and Eric lost. So he became the spinner while Alec remained the pace bowler. Innocent and starry-eyed, they joined the Surrey XI staff in 1938. When war stopped play, they joined the RAF, where their days were brightened by the general inability of officers to tell them apart. Serving in France in 1940, they were somewhat taken aback when someone knelt at their feet: local superstition had it that identical twins were lucky. In 1943 they were both offered promotion to warrant officer, but rather than be parted, they agreed that only one of them should take it, and they would share the extra pay. This time Eric won the toss and accepted the promotion.

There is a nice story about Alec having a haircut on tour in Sydney. Ten minutes later Eric walked into the same barber's. 'Cripes, it hasn't taken your hair long to grow again,' said the bemused barber. And on a boat to South Africa a woman fond of pink gins thought she had had one too many when she saw them together for the first time.

Eric could never understand the suggestions, frequently made, that he might be envious of Alec's greater success (Eric never made it to the England side, though he was a stalwart all-rounder in the Surrey XI). Eric is the elder twin by ten minutes, and this could account for his mature attitude. Alec says, in his rather orotund style:

> We have always worked together in complete harmony and many is the time I have thought it unfair that the fruits of our joint endeavours should have sometimes fallen to me alone. It would have been intolerable if Eric had shown the slightest hint of resentment or reminded me that so much had hinged on the flip of a coin. Eric and not I might have received the OBE and later the CBE ... I owe much to my other half, and if it is deemed that I served the game, then cricket also is in his debt.

Perhaps the most striking thing about identical twins is the way they complement each other. It is obvious that they are two halves of a whole.

The aptly named pop duo Gemini, a.k.a. David and Michael Smallwood, are identical twins from Birmingham. They are twenty-two and have been on the pop scene since 1994 – they were successful performers before their debut single 'Even Though You Broke My Heart' was released to considerable acclaim by EMI, who signed them up as soon as they heard them.

They now live in Ealing, west London, but were brought up in Smethwick by opera-singing parents: the family's musical background goes back a couple of generations. Great-Gran was a pianist; Grandpa was a piano-tuner, while Gran sang and played the piano in the Birmingham Town Hall for the troops during the war. She is the boys' 'greatest influence'. By the age of four, Michael could play the piano and David could play classical guitar. They both studied music at college – Michael the piano and David the drums, for which he holds a teacher's diploma. The pop stars they revere and wish to emulate are George Michael, Madonna and especially Michael Jackson.

David is twenty minutes older than Michael, and they both agree that he is the one who 'holds back a little'. He is also the one who says that as well as love, 'you need support and to be understood, which isn't the same thing as love', whereas all Michael needs in addition to love is 'self-fulfilment'. Obviously very close – they describe themselves as a 'double-yolker' – they are identical to the extent that Michael, who is obviously the more mischievous, was able to go off with David's girlfriend once. 'She didn't know for an hour, even after we'd kissed,' he said.

The Smallwoods are keen football fans, but support different teams, David Manchester United and Michael Wolverhampton Wanderers. When they were young, one of Michael's ambitions was to be a tennis professional (he had played for Shropshire as a boy) while David's was strictly musical: he wanted to be the 'best drummer in the world'.

Even in the murky world of politics, identical twins collaborate rather than compete. And if the elder twin succeeds earlier than the younger one, he will give his brother the support and encouragement to enable him to make it too.

Angela Eagle, the Labour MP for Wallasey in Cheshire, was elected in April 1992. Not only was she the first Labour candidate to win Wallasey, but in so doing she ousted the minister for overseas development, Lynda Chalker. In her maiden speech, Eagle paid tribute to the new Baroness Chalker as a 'formidable opponent' and a 'popular and well-respected' former MP who had 'served Wallasey well'. It is rather ironic that as a fourteen-year-old schoolgirl she had questioned Lynda Chalker at a Hansard Society meeting about the future of the House of Lords.

Angela has an identical twin, Maria, who is a solicitor in Liverpool. They were born in Bridlington, where their mother was a seamstress and their father worked in the printing trade. Angela joined the Crosby Labour Party when she was seventeen and at Oxford, where she read politics, philosophy and economics, she became chairman of the university Fabian Society. She has been described as tough-minded, loyal and articulate – a punchy young ex-trade union official, and a parliamentary feminist who wants Parliament to 'move with the times if we are not to atrophy into some quaint but irrelevant sideshow, fit only for tourists to admire'. She started out as a researcher for COHSE, then moved on to become press officer and then parliamentary liaison officer.

At the time she was selected as candidate for the marginal seat of Wallasey, her twin sister, also a keen Labour Party member, was simultaneously chosen to contest nearby Crosby, the Eagles' home constituency. Maria was defeated (as one of her predecessors, Tony Blair's wife Cherie Booth, had been), but was subsequently selected to stand for Liverpool Garston, where the Labour majority is 12,000. Maria says of her MP sister: 'She's more pragmatic than I am and tremendously determined; she's always had the edge on me in concentration.' This was demonstrated in her skill at chess, which the twins started playing when they were seven. They went on to play for Lancashire, and Angela became British girls' champion. Both girls also played cricket for the county. They have remained very close, and say they are not only twins but also best friends. Angela says of Maria: 'She will always stand up for a principle. She is very brave and goes in feet first with boots flying. After several years in the trades union movement, I'm more inclined to stand back and consider what can be salvaged from a situation.'

When I asked a colleague of hers which was the elder twin, she said she could guess. Angela, eldest by fifteen minutes, seems to have that little bit more authority and conviction than her sister.

Although only one twin can be dominant, in the sporting world, too, as we have seen with the Bedser twins, support and collaboration can best be supplied by the person who is closest to you, literally, your other half.

Henry Cooper, one of the best-loved figures in the history of British boxing, won three Lonsdale belts outright. He held, in turn, the British, European and Commonwealth heavyweight championships, and was renowned for his left hook – "Enery's 'ammer' – among everyone in the fight game. He used it to floor the then Cassius Clay (now Muhammad Ali) at Wembley in 1963, though he was himself forced to retire in the next round. He won forty of his fifty-five bouts, retiring after losing on a controversial points decision to Joe Bugner at Wembley in March 1971.

Since his retirement, Henry has remained a much-loved figure as a Fabergé front man for Brut, a charity organizer, a fanatical golfer, supermarket-opener, Water Rat, TV personality – the list is endless.

His wife, Albina, is Italian, and they have two sons, Henry Marco and John Pietro. He also has an identical twin brother, George, who has shared with him all his triumphs and failures. Henry recalls how they used to look like two peas in a pod, 'although in our business you get your features altered a bit over the years. Still, even these days, we can just about get away with the identical twin trick for a couple of minutes.'

In his autobiography, Henry pays a moving tribute to his brother.

I have many reasons to thank George. In the beginning, at the Lying-In Hospital in York Road, Westminster, on 3 May 1934, I was only born because George was there to help push me out and I arrived in the world twenty minutes before he did. Then, for twenty-six years, we were constantly together, at school, in the army, and in boxing. We each started out with our own fight careers, and then George retired, but he didn't quit the game. He started his own business as a plastering contractor and then, in the last three or four years of my career, whenever I had a fight he would let others take care of the business for three or four weeks while he came to help me and be my trainer. He was a ready-made sparring partner as well. In fact he helped out in a dozen important ways. We always went away during that time and George and I lived together for twenty-four hours a day, just like we had done in Bellingham [their childhood home]. When I got up in the morning to do the road work, George was there on the bike; after training, he gave me a rub-down and we would spend the whole day together. Then, on the big night, he was always in my corner. So, although he has always stood back a little while I have been in the limelight, I know that without George and his encouragement I would not have achieved half the things I have managed to do.

Henry and George are still close, as are their families.

The Gibbons twins' story shows that the powerful bonding that exists between twins, the sense of being two halves of the same person, can have a destructive effect if they are allowed to become too inward-looking.

June and Jennifer Gibbons, who became known as the Silent Twins, were the daughters of a couple from Barbados and were brought up in RAF quarters around Britain. Their father had left Barbados when he was twenty and eventually became an assistant air-controller. There were three other children in the family, an elder brother and sister and a younger sister.

June Alison was the elder twin, Jennifer Lorraine arriving ten minutes later. For the first three years of their lives they were happy, laughing children, just like any other toddlers. They both had a slight speech impediment, which made it difficult for their parents to understand them, and this, perhaps, is where the seeds of their silence were sown, as Marjorie Wallace, who was very much involved with them, describes in her biography, *The Silent Twins*.

Once they started going to school their teachers, too, found it difficult to understand them. Their reports contained comments like, 'June is beginning to write, but still lacks confidence to speak or read.' They would make signs to each other and look at each other before answering a question, which prompted the assessment, 'They tend to be too content to do very little. They show very little initiative or imagination.' It was clearly frustrating for their teachers.

Their father was posted to another town when they were eight and a half and they moved to a new school. It was less friendly, and June and Jennifer were laughed at, bullied and baited. They stood out not only because they were twins, and because of their behaviour, but also because of their colour – there were very few other black children in the school. They clung to each other and withdrew even more from the hostile world. By now they spoke to virtually no one but each other and communicated with their parents by writing notes. The excuse their mother made to herself was that they were very shy and still suffered from their speech impediment.

The twins had speech therapy, but to no avail. At their next school an education therapist was assigned to them to help overcome whatever it was that was causing their self-imposed isolation. Again, the treatment had very little effect. In one of their written replies to questions put by the therapist, June wrote: 'First of all let's get one thing straight: nobody knows us really. All these things you say about us are all wrong. Nobody really knows what goes on between us two. We may be twins, but we are different twins.'

This was the root of the trouble. Jennifer, ten minutes younger, felt inferior, less loved by her parents, less favoured by her teachers and believed she had fewer recognized talents. She wanted to take June back with her into the womb, to the time before the egg from which they had developed had split, to remove any discernible differences so that they were, in effect, one human being. June, on the other hand, longed to be different, to be the prettier, cleverer twin, the one people loved and admired. She said later that she had thought about trying to drown Jennifer in the river so that she would be free. But she could not survive alone, and all attempts to separate them were resisted by both twins. Life was unbearable together, but unbearable apart. It was an insoluble situation.

The story ended in tragedy. Following a bizarre episode in which, apparently drunk, they set fire to a shed in the garden, they were charged and found guilty of arson. The only suitable secure place to which they could be sent was Broadmoor. They had already received treatment in two institutions, but Broadmoor was more than just an institution, it was a prison. Their parents were shocked but helpless, says Wallace.

The girls thought Broadmoor would be enjoyable and talked of 'drinking lemonade on the lawn'. In fact they were separated and their doors were locked. Visitors had to sign in and out and other inmates, like Peter Sutcliffe, the Yorkshire Ripper, might be found at the disco. They were diagnosed and given medication which included tranquillizers. These made them more relaxed and at last they began to talk to other people.

Five years and several court hearings later, it was decided that June and Jennifer should be released. By now they were thirty. They were due to return to the outside world via a rehabilitation centre, the Caswell Clinic in Bridgend. The day before the move, Jennifer said she felt a bit tired and went to lie down. Less than twenty-four hours later she was dead. The doctors said her death had been caused by inflammation of the heart muscle and was very unusual.

June was completely devastated. She says that at the time she thought her life was finished too, and that she would never get over her sister's death. That was three years ago. She is now settled in Haverfordwest and has even been back to Barbados to visit relatives. She admits that their lives as twins were 'one big mess. But day by day I'm getting out of it. I'm ten times stronger than I was and I'm living for both of us. One more day for me is one more day for my sister. I'm still a twin. Born a twin, die a twin.' And she kneels at her sister's grave and says, 'Hello, Jenny, I've brought you some flowers.'

The death of any sibling has an effect which lasts a lifetime, but the death of a twin is particularly devastating for the surviving one. Joan Woodward, who is now nearly seventy, lost her identical twin, Pamela, to meningitis when they were three.

My parents had been so proud of us. My mother used to say it was wonderful pushing the pram down the

King's Road with these tiny blue-eyed, auburn-haired babies in it. Everybody stopped to look ... I always felt I could never make it up to her. It has been the major thrust in my life, the feeling that I can never be quite good enough. I have spent all my time on this task which is doomed to failure.

Joan is a psychotherapist and the author of an important piece of research on lone twins which led to the establishment of the Lone Twin Network. Their register, which has more than three hundred members, is kept by Clare Fay, another lone twin, whose sister Lizzie died nearly eight years ago. The address of the Lone Twin Network is: c/o The Multiple Births Foundation, Queen Charlotte's and Chelsea Hospital, Goldhawk Road, London W6 OXG (0181-740 3519). Anybody who feels in need of support is welcome to contact them.

To be a twin, especially an identical twin, is clearly a life-defining experience. The examples described here suggest that twins often have a love-hate relationship, not just with each other, but with the whole business of being twins. As children they may enjoy the special status accorded to identical twins; they may even enjoy being stared at and talked about. But they often come to resent being treated as a single unit, both at home and at school, and suffer from the loss of intimacy, even affection, that goes with that lack of differentiation. Their oneness is a blessing in the remarkable, even telepathic rapport they feel for each other, but a curse in that they are not accepted as individuals.

There comes a time, evidently a very painful one, when twins must decide how widely to separate their paths and how to build up their own lives and identities. Although fraternal twins face some of the handicaps and dilemmas, these come in much more diluted form than they do with identical twins.

Perhaps the most surprising aspect of twin relationships is the significance of birth order. The gap may be measured only in minutes, but it is just as important as one of years and months.

8 Adopted Children

To adopt a child requires courage, for it is both a delicate and a hazardous thing to do. It is a testing experience, particularly where other children, adopted or biological, are involved, because of its impact on the family birth order.

It is generally agreed nowadays that everything should be done to help a mother and child to stay together. Accordingly there is no longer the same stigma attached to single mothers or illegitimate children and consequently fewer adoptions. Another aspect of the importance now given to biological mother-and-child relationships is that it is accepted that in later life an adopted child may want to make contact with his biological parents. These are likely to be described in politically correct circles as 'birth' parents rather than 'natural' parents, which might imply that adoptive parents are in some way unnatural.

The most common family pattern in adoption involves a single child being adopted by older parents who have tried for some time to have children of their own. Having finally come to terms with the fact that this is not going to happen, they feel they are too old by this stage to cope with more than one child.

For parents who have not been through childbearing and birth, the experience of bringing up a child is every bit as beset with difficulties as it is for those who have experienced the full cycle. The hurdles will be all the higher if great care is not taken in matching the birth and adoptive parents and their achievements and backgrounds. It would be a mismatch if, for example, a bright child were adopted by dim, insensitive parents. It is all too tempting for people in that situation to abuse their power, perhaps by telling their adopted child: 'You wouldn't be here if it wasn't for us.'

Difficulties liable to arise from adoption include the child's shame at being adopted, which may be aggravated by a feeling that she has been rejected by her birth mother. 'Why did she give me away? Because she didn't love me.'

The adoptive parents, for their part, are likely to be nervous about telling the child she is adopted for fear of being subsequently rejected as parents themselves. They may also continue to suffer from feelings of inadequacy resulting from their own infertility.

In a 'mixed' family, that is, one which includes biological and adopted children, there is a constant danger of the parents' behaviour being misinterpreted. An adopted child tends to give more than a biological child to her parents because of her feelings of insecurity and need for love. If she cannot do this, she may well walk out of the relationship.

Virtually any pattern of family life will be affected by adoption. If, for example, the first child is adopted and then a biological child is born, the characteristic dethronement of the eldest child is likely to be felt more strongly than it is by a biological first-born. And this situation happens surprisingly frequently – there was even a time when couples who had difficulty conceiving were advised to adopt 'to get the machinery working'. Another trait of the adopted child is that he is likely to suspect that preferential treatment is being given to the mother's own child or children, especially if he comes after one or more biological children. And as adopted children have a much greater fear of being deprived of love, there is even more sibling rivalry between adopted siblings, or adopted and biological siblings, than between biological siblings alone. If parents die, or cannot cope because of illness, children are often brought up by grandparents, or uncles and aunts.

One of the most famous of the Greek myths is the story of an adoption that went catastrophically wrong. Oedipus was the son of King Laius of Thebes and Queen Jocasta. When it was prophesied that Laius would be slain by his own son, the baby was left to die on a mountainside. He was found by a shepherd and given to King Polybus of Corinth, who adopted him, pretending he was his own child. When Oedipus grew up he was told in a prophecy that he would kill his father and marry his mother. Not knowing that he was adopted, he thought this applied to his adoptive parents, so he left Corinth to avoid so grisly an outcome. On his travels he met and killed Laius by accident and arrived at Thebes, where he rid the city of the monster Sphinx. His reward was the hand of the widowed queen, Jocasta. Eventually it was discovered that they were mother and son and that he had killed his own father. Jocasta took her own life, while Oedipus blinded himself and went into exile.

*

Fortunately the experiences of most adoptive couples and adopted children are a great deal less extreme. But the hazards are considerable, as a few examples may show. Take the case of an American couple who adopted a baby and then produced one of their own. Ralph and Natalie were a cosmopolitan couple: he was an engineer who had worked all over the world, including London, Hamburg and the Far East, from a base in Chicago; she was a designer, who often travelled to Paris and Milan. Like most couples, they wanted a family, but although doctors pronounced them both fit and capable, they just did not conceive. After ten years of marriage, they decided to adopt a child. They were both dark-haired but fair-skinned. The baby, Philip, had enormous brown eyes and a dark complexion. As he grew up, he became almost swarthy and it became more and more obvious to the outside world that he was not their own child.

They loved Philip dearly and spoiled him outrageously. Then, when he was about six years old, Natalie became pregnant. She was by then a 'mature' mother-to-be, but all went well and a large healthy baby boy, Luke, was born. Both she and Ralph were thrilled with this unexpected gift.

Philip, however, was naturally very upset and although they tried very hard to reassure him and show him how much they loved him, the dethroned prince found it difficult to accept his little brother. Luke inherited the family looks and was so obviously their son that the already apparent difference between Philip and his parents was even more marked.

Ten years later, Luke is a bright, intelligent, attractive

boy, while Philip is a mixed-up teenager whose appearance now reveals his Middle Eastern origins.

Fortunately, Ralph and Natalie have a large apartment so the two boys can have their own space. At one stage they thought they would have to send Philip away to school, fearing that he might be too aggressive with Luke. However, realizing this would be the ultimate rejection, they managed to avoid any such drastic action.

Luke is a well-adjusted boy, and, like all younger brothers, he teases Philip, and is perhaps aware that he has a slight advantage. This inevitably leads to friction. His parents bend over backwards to make sure that Philip feels as loved and wanted as Luke, but sometimes it is difficult. When the boys are older, the situation will undoubtedly improve, but meanwhile they are all suffering.

The following couple were in the reverse situation. They had one child and wanted another, but had been advised against it on medical grounds.

Elspeth and Jack are a kind, civilized couple, nearing retirement age. Their first child, a son, is gentle, pleasant, reliable and very much like Jack. A year after Elspeth was told she should not have any more children, they decided to adopt, partly because they didn't want their son to be lonely or under pressure later on, and partly because they longed for a daughter. Janet, two and a quarter years younger than their boy, was born to impecunious students who found they couldn't manage. They had put her up for adoption reluctantly, but were greatly relieved when a suitable home was found.

Elspeth and Jack were delighted with the new baby, their son less so. But he soon adjusted to the new arrival and it seemed that they now had the perfect family. Janet was a very bright, lively, rather aggressive little girl, and as she grew older she became, as Elspeth described it, 'a bit of a handful'. She knew she was adopted and used this information cleverly. If she was refused a sixth eclair on the grounds that she would be sick, she would immediately say, 'It's because I'm adopted, isn't it?' The son seemed to take it in his stride and only once did he make a riposte to this frequent accusation. 'Well, I don't know,' he said, 'but I'm glad I'm not!' His parents were furious and forbade him to say anything like that again.

Janet was furious too, and she used the incident to manipulate her adoptive parents. 'I lost count of the number of times she threatened to run away,' sighs Elspeth, who was the one who bore the brunt of Janet's tantrums. These continued throughout her schooldays. Elspeth was several times summoned by the form mistress, who complained that her daughter was disruptive and rebellious, albeit extremely bright. Once Janet went away to university things began to calm down, although tension persisted between her and her adoptive mother. She is now married and has two children of her own, and at last, says Elspeth, 'I think we've got there.' Janet is still volatile and argumentative, but she has more understanding now of what a difficult time she gave her adoptive mother.

An Italian couple living in London had a similar experience to Ralph and Natalie's, but in their case it had a different outcome. These prospective parents, too,

were well-travelled, sophisticated people who had unsuc-
cessfully tried to start a family of their own. Their local
priest put them in touch with an adoption agency, and
six months later they became the proud parents of twin
girls.

Joanne and Laura were extremely easy babies in
themselves, but being twins they were hard work. Everywhere their parents went they were admired and cooed
over. There were no problems with physical incompatibility. The parents were in any case of contrasting
appearance – the husband was darkish and stocky, the
wife was slim and fair – and the twins were fair-skinned
with mousey brown hair.

Three years after Joanne and Laura were adopted, just
when their mother began to feel relaxed after the
anxieties of rearing two babies, she finally became
pregnant. A boy was born. John was a lovely baby, but
he had Down's syndrome. The parents were overjoyed
to have their own baby, but felt the combination of guilt
and helplessness experienced by most parents who have
produced a child with this condition. Fortunately, the
mother was able to give the baby lots of attention to
assuage her feelings of guilt, as the twins were by now at
nursery school.

As Joanne and Laura grew up, they adored their little
brother and were highly protective towards him. The
parents soon came to terms with the limitations John's
condition imposed, and, like many Down's syndrome
children, he was extremely happy and lovable. John's
birth changed their lives, of course, but he is contented
and making good progress at the special-needs school he
attends, while the twins are flourishing at theirs. The

help their brother needs has deflected any possible jealousy the twins might have felt towards him, and the family grew closer as a result of what they thought at first was a tragedy.

In other circumstances, adoption can, however, take a heavy toll on a family's biological children. The Wilsons are a kind, caring couple with active social consciences. They involve themselves in the community and both contribute greatly to the activities of their local church.

John is a talented architect, an easy-going and relaxed person; his wife, Catherine, has an almost saintly aura. She is always solicitous and anxious to help anyone with a problem, and has taken a special counselling course to equip her to visit lonely and sometimes terminally ill patients at her local hospital.

They have two children of their own: Sarah, now twenty-eight and a doctor, and Jack, twenty-six, who has followed his father into architecture. Feeling that they were privileged to have such happy and fulfilling lives, they wanted to share some of this good fortune with someone less advantaged, and so they adopted two children. There was a gap of two years between Paul and Jeannie, the adopted children, and Paul was three and half years younger than Jack. Paul's biological mother was Indian and his father a West Indian from St Kitt's. Jeannie's young parents were from Jamaica.

'Paul was difficult from the word go,' said Catherine. 'We didn't know it then, but he suffered with ADHD [Attention Deficient Hyperactive Disorder], caused by a chemical in the brain. He just didn't fit in. We tried everything. We took him to see all kinds of specialists, but nobody could sort him out.' Paul felt the rejection by his biological parents very keenly, and Catherine recalls that when he was young, he would often swear, 'If I ever find her, I'll kill her.' Catherine tried to reassure him that he would understand better when he was older.

When Jeannie was four, Catherine gave birth to a baby boy, Joe. This new arrival destabilized the adopted children a little, but they soon settled down again.

Paul had been going to the local school which Sarah and Jack had attended, but at fourteen he walked out and refused to go back. He had already been picked up by the police for joyriding. Not long afterwards, Catherine gave birth to another baby boy. With six children, they felt their family was complete, but life was not all sweetness and light because of Paul's behaviour. There was an incident involving drugs, the police and angry scenes. At one stage a knife was even produced.

'Sarah, my daughter, was very good at defusing these situations. She was able to calm Paul down. But once she had gone away to college, the other children did suffer. Paul thought that Jeannie should be like him because she was adopted. He called drugs "my culture",' Catherine explains. But Jeannie was not interested and soon learned to stand up to Paul's bullying. The other child affected was Joe, who was about ten by this time. He too started to refuse to go to school – but not because he was rebellious or disaffected. 'We discovered that he was worried about leaving me and the baby alone in the house while Paul was around,' says Catherine. 'If a row started, he would scoop up the baby and whisk him up to the bedroom.'

The two older children, Sarah and Jack, were typical

first- and second-borns, but any sibling rivalry that might have existed between them was dissipated by Paul's behaviour. Sarah felt responsible for Paul, but Jack went his own way and spent a lot of time with his friends.

'Paul did have a disruptive effect, I must admit,' says Catherine, 'and once Sarah left home and had more of a perspective, she was very angry at what Paul had done to the family.'

The story had a tragic but perhaps predictable ending. Not long ago Paul, aged twenty-two, came home from a rehabilitation centre and went off to see the mother of two children he had fathered. They went to a nearby park, sat under a tree, took a cocktail of drugs and went to sleep. The young mother awoke some time later, but Paul did not.

Catherine feels that, at least at that moment, Paul was happy with life. For the rest of the family, the sadness of his death seems to be tinged with guilt and relief. 'Jeannie, now off to music college in Manchester, was sad, but also a little relieved,' says Catherine, 'and Joe, who is now back into the routine of school again, is also more relaxed and happy.'

Jeannie had already become the middle child of the family, the odd one out, and Catherine thinks this is partly due to Paul's earlier attempts to encourage her to feel alienated from the family. At the time she resisted, but now that she is the only adopted child, the characteristic middle-child feelings of isolation are emphasized. The two older biological children are close, as are the two younger ones. But Catherine is confident that Jeannie is secure enough to know that she is a vital part of the family.

*

One of the co-ordinators of the Parent-to-Parent Information on Adoption Service, Roger Fenton, believes that adopted children may find it helpful and encouraging as well as interesting to know how many famous people are adopted. Although many high achievers do not want to publicize their adoptive status, some make no secret of it. After much research and validation of data and confidentiality, Mr Fenton has compiled a substantial list, which is available from him at Lower Boddington, Daventry, Northampton, NN11 6YB.

Among those on Mr Fenton's register is Kate Adie, the well-known chief news correspondent of the BBC, who was named Reporter of the Year three years ago. Her mother became pregnant when her husband was away at war in the Royal Army Medical Corps in India, and put Kate up for adoption as a baby.

She became the much-loved only child of a couple called Maud and John Adie, who lived in Sunderland and with whom she had a very happy childhood. Maud, whom she adored, died in 1990, aged seventy-eight. John, a pharmacist, is still alive, and lives in a Sunderland nursing home.

The Adies sent Kate to the private Sunderland Church High School, where she worked hard and made many friends. She went on to Newcastle University, where she read Swedish and Old Icelandic. Watching Kate on TV, the determination and single-mindedness of the only child is instantly recognizable. She is also self-confident and gives the impression of being organized and efficient. Kate Adie has shown plenty of another only-child characteristic, self-sufficiency, in her professional life, not least when faced with desert wastes and mountain snows, usually as the only female in the television crew.

Kate had been curious for many years about her original father and mother, but had not embarked on any kind of quest for fear of hurting her adoptive parents. With her mother dead and father in a nursing home, however, she felt it would be possible. After much searching, she found not only her birth mother, but also an older sister and a younger brother and sister. So now, as well as being an only child, she is the second-born in a family of four.

Another well-known personality writes in his autobiograhy about adoption. Brian Moore, a City solicitor and rugby player who has played at the top level for Harlequins and England, was said to be one of the most terrifying figures in British sport: hence his affectionate nickname, Pit Bull.

Brian's birth mother was a very young teacher from Birmingham, his birth father a Chinese dentist. His father had gone away, and life for a young unmarried mother in Birmingham in the sixties seemed neither socially acceptable nor financially feasible to his mother.

Brian was adopted by Ralph and Dorothy Moore, who both came from families of five children themselves and were committed Methodists. When he arrived there were already two daughters, Catherine and Elizabeth, and an adopted daughter, Ai Lien, all older than Brian. So for a while he was the baby. Then came a younger boy, Paul, and another older girl, Gwen, and he ended up as the second youngest in a family of six. Tough though that may sound, the Moores evidently knew what they were doing. Brian says he could not have wished for better, more understanding parents if he had chosen them himself, and he feels they handled him incredibly well when he was young. Both he and Paul were young tearaways, but Brian was particularly aggressive, probably because he had four older sisters and had to attract attention somehow. But his parents kept Paul on a tighter rein than Brian because they realized that Brian's aggression needed some release; Paul, on the other hand, was just being a typical, perverse teenager and the somewhat spoiled baby of the family.

Brian had been curious for a long time to know more about his birth mother, but did nothing because his adoptive parents had gently discouraged him, for fear that he would be disappointed. In his thirties he realized that she would probably now be in her fifties, and the thought that she might die, if indeed she were still alive, without him having met her prompted him to action. Using one of the private detectives in his office, he started trying to trace her, and before long had her name, address and telephone number. Yet he was apprehensive: this could prove to be a second rejection. Was his birth an episode she had hoped to forget? Eventually contact was made through a third party to avoid embarrassment and they met one day at his home in Twickenham. At first neither knew what to say, but gradually the encounter became easier. She asked him if he could forgive her and he said that he could, and told her what wonderful parents the Moores had been. This made her feel better. Brian discovered he had a younger brother and sister and that, far from being at the tail end of the family, in his birth family he was the first-born. As far as Brian is concerned, the Moores are his mum and dad and always will be, but he does not regret finding his birth mother and hopes the relationship will gradually grow and be mutually beneficial.

Another happy adopted child is Dame Kiri Te Kanawa, the world-famous New Zealand-born singer, who went on to adopt her own children. She was adopted as a baby by a Maori man and European wife, a couple of the same ethnic backgrounds as her birth parents. Her adoptive mother was musical and soon realized that their child had a special talent. Kiri was an only child, and so her parents were able to concentrate on her. They arranged singing lessons for her, and eventually her mother brought her to England to work with a well-known singing teacher.

Like so many only children, Kiri was given the attention and support to fulfil her promise – as well as the expectations of her adoptive parents. She also had the only child's self-confidence, ability to work hard and determination to succeed, which she has done at the highest level in a ferociously competitive field.

She and her husband, Australian businessman Desmond Park, who eventually became her manager, were unable to have their own children. They decided that, as Kiri had had such a good experience of adoption, they would adopt themselves. Perhaps because Kiri had at times been lonely as a child, they adopted two, a boy and a girl: Antonia is now nearly twenty and Thomas will soon be eighteen. Few parents can understand better than Kiri the fears and insecurities that adopted children feel. So many are afraid their adoptive parents will grow tired of them, and that if they are naughty, they will be sent away, but Antonia and Thomas have had the distinct advantage of a mother who understands these feelings.

As these cases show, both adopting a child and being adopted yourself can be a hazardous business. Couples who already have one or more children are ostensibly best equipped to cope with an addition to the family from outside, but on the other hand the arrival of an adoptive child will disrupt the existing family pattern and is liable to be much resented by the parents' biological children. The adoptive child is in turn likely to feel like a second-class citizen if given the slightest cause for resentment.

That deep sense of vulnerability is often aggravated if adoption is followed by the birth of a biological child who will enjoy the double advantage of being the youngest and the parents' own flesh and blood. A child already rejected by its own mother now fears rejection by its adoptive parents. No wonder adopted children feel such a desperate need to be reassured that they are loved. Yet on the positive side, a great many adoptions prove intensely rewarding for both sides.

9 Step-Families

Many of us were brought up on stories of the trials and tribulations of the unfortunate Snow White, Hansel and Gretel and Cinderella. Traditionally, step-parents have rated somewhere between witches and mothers-in-law in the bad-press stakes. Everyone sympathizes with the children, but step-families are made up of more than one side, and that is what sets them apart. The cast of characters is confusing and various. There's the natural parent, the step-parent, the natural parent's children, the step-parent's children, the children from the union of step-parent and parent, relatives and step-relatives, even the dog and the step-dog!

According to the National Step-Family Association, the number of step-families has increased with the rise in divorce. Their statistics suggest that one in five children under the age of eighteen is living in a step-family. Step-family self-help groups are being set up around the country and problems are nowadays acknowledged and dealt with more openly. This is partly due to a gradual change in the public's attitude, one result of which is that the old stigma associated with step-families has disappeared.

In this new, more tolerant climate of opinion it is accepted that there are no definitive guidelines to follow to achieve the perfect step-family. Step-parents and children have to invent their relationships as they go along. Each family will have different experiences and backgrounds. It may prove relevant that one family is very musical, another sports-orientated and yet another more intellectual. Horizons may have been widened by travel; or, by contrast, long residence in the same house, surrounded by old friends, may have provided one side of the new, joined family with a valuable sense of security.

Combining two families into one is obviously difficult. For the children involved, loss of a seemingly established place in the family is often hard to accept. Having been recognized as ruler of the roost, the first-born might be dethroned by an older step-sibling rather than experiencing the usual displacement by a younger brother or sister. Or the pecking order might be changed for the baby, whom everyone has adored and spoiled, when a younger step-sibling is introduced into the family. The upheaval is likely to be most devastating for an only child.

William Beer explains in *Strangers in the House* that five main patterns of change in birth order are possible when children are combined in a step-family: an only child becomes the oldest child; an only child becomes the youngest child; an only child becomes the middle child; an oldest child becomes a middle child; a youngest child becomes a middle child.

The most common characteristics seen in half- and step-children are inadequacy or aggression in the face of competition and, following that, insecurity arising from different backgrounds. The changes in the family dynamics can bring out leadership qualities and feelings of responsibility if the new family is young, but resentment and withdrawal if there is a displacement problem. There is an important difference between step-siblings, who have no common parent, and half-siblings, who do. Displacement can still occur, but it is much less likely to do so where there is a common mother or father than with two separate sets of parents.

Mothers are usually given custody of children, especially if the children are young. Often they then add to their first family, and here there is no displacement as such. But there may be another form of displacement.

Take the case of Sue, who was married to a British academic and living in Rome when she met Peter. She had two daughters, then eight and ten, and brought them back to London with her when she returned to be with Peter. They eventually married and had two daughters of their own. The age gap between the two sets of girls was about thirteen years, and the younger of the elder set became virtually a little mother to the younger two.

The first of the elder daughters is a brilliant mathematician who teaches in both the United States and the UK. She was always a little nervous, and had an endearing slight lisp, while the second was warm, plumpish and jolly with a strong maternal streak, and not as academically inclined, although she became a successful and well-loved primary school teacher.

Of their half-sisters, the elder was again clever, studying architecture and desperate to succeed: she knew her father had always wanted to be an architect, even though he had in fact done well for himself in computer software.

She is now a talented architect, but a little anxious and somewhat insecure, according to her mother. The baby of the family was always bright and rather cheeky with lots of common sense. She is now very much her own woman. Having graduated in psychology, she is more interested in dealing with the practical side of children with problems than with the more academic psychoanalysis her mother had hoped for.

Both sets of daughters follow the first- and second-born pattern: the first in each case being a high achiever and the second a more relaxed enjoyer of life. But the two-families-in-one set-up led to some complications. Although there was little jealousy within either pair of daughters, it did raise its head – albeit in unspoken form – between the two sets. Because Peter was far more successful in financial terms than Sue's first husband, there was a lot more money available for the second two than there had been for the first. Peter was always very generous with his stepdaughters, but they had missed out for perhaps fifteen years and saw their half-sisters having more or less everything they wanted.

Furthermore, the eldest of the four daughters had been very close to her mother, particularly when they first came to England, playing not exactly a husband's role, but certainly a very supportive and protective one. Even though she has now married and has small children of her own, it has been difficult for her to cut the umbilical cord. As a result, her relationship with her stepfather has tended to be somewhat tense and almost competitive. This made her not so much unhappy as emotionally uncomfortable. She once told her mother that although she was very fond of Peter, he wasn't 'blood'.

So instead of the eldest playing the 'little mother', a role which would have come naturally in a first family with much younger siblings, that part was left to the second-born child, who was adored by her young half-sisters.

These three are very close, despite the age gap, whereas the eldest has, after years of toing and froing, decided to settle in the US. It is, she feels, the only way she can resolve the relationship with her mother.

For stepmothers, keeping calm and rolling with the punches is often the best way of dealing with a potentially fraught situation. Caroline is the mother of Tom, aged eight, and Ruth, aged six. She is also stepmother to Charlie, who is twelve. To an outsider, the family seems doomed to serious difficulties, and life has certainly not been easy. But Caroline has great common sense and compassion, with some training as a social worker as well. Her husband shares her gift for dealing with potential family disasters with loving yet objective understanding.

Charlie has been spending part of his life with his stepmother and father since he was two. Although the pattern changes from time to time, he generally spends weekdays with his step-family and the weekend with his mother during term-time, reversing this arrangement in the holidays.

The three children are affected in different ways by this lifestyle. When he is with his mother, Charlie has to be almost a small adult, since she has her own business and often not as much time to spend with him as she'd like. When he returns to his step-family, it is not unusual for him to take out the resultant anger and resentment on his young half-siblings or his stepmother. Although a typical first-born natural leader, he has to re-establish himself and stamp his authority on the larger family each time he returns. Tom, his half-brother, also has readjustments to make. When Charlie is around, Tom is happy to accept his authority, but as soon as Charlie goes to his 'other home', Tom becomes the leader and Ruth the follower.

On their own, Tom and Ruth are very much a pair, first- and second-born, sometimes playing together, sometimes fighting. But when Charlie returns, the pairings change. Charlie and Ruth get on quite well, often having giggling fits together which leave Tom as a temporary monkey in the middle. On other occasions, Charlie and Tom do boyish things together, playing football or rugby, and Ruth is the odd one out. The gender factor is involved here too: Caroline says she has far more 'sorting out' to do when the three of them are together than when there are just two.

As the age gap is relatively large, Charlie is not as yet too threatened by Tom. However, Tom's academic potential looks greater then Charlie's: the older boy is bright, but perhaps because his primary-school education suffered from all the toing and froing, he has difficulty concentrating. Tom, who is also intelligent, is beginning to catch up with him, and an element of competition is entering the relationship.

There are problems ahead, but fortunately for all of them, Caroline is optimistic that 'it will all work out'.

In another step-family, the first-born has not been shown such understanding by his stepmother. At fifteen years old, Robert, a rather shy only child, was introduced to his stepmother, 'who took an instant dislike to me and from then on treated me like an unwanted dog'. His father was a brilliant but absentminded art historian who didn't mean to neglect him, but succeeded in doing so comprehensively. Later on, when he went on trips abroad, he would bring back presents for his second family, Robert's half-siblings, but forget all about his eldest child, by then nineteen or twenty.

Because of the huge age gap there was virtually no sibling rivalry between Robert and his young brothers and sister. He was very much an only child – self-sufficient, hard-working and perhaps emotionally imma-ture. The eldest of the siblings was also hard-working, conscientious and responsible, a typical first-born, and he and Robert got along well. The second was not so easy. Rather attention-seeking, flamboyant and with a lot of charm, he was his mother's obvious favourite, which made life difficult for both Robert and Bruce. The last child, a girl, adored Robert and used to follow him around.

Big brother tried hard to be accepted by his young siblings and they responded well. There was never any tension between them, in spite of the 'wicked step-mother', who undoubtedly tried to stir up bad blood. Robert remembers how once, after a row, his stepmother told him to pack his bag and go. As he was doing so, one by one, his half-brothers and -sister came to apologize to him.

Sadly, he has never resolved his relationship with his stepmother, and although he has never stopped trying, it looks as if he never will, for she is now in her eighties and suffering from a terminal illness.

It is when there is no common father or mother, and two sets of children with their own fathers and mothers are brought together, often unwillingly, in the hope that they will 'get on', that problems are at their most acute.

Sally and Nick, both Australian, had lived in London all their married lives and had two sons, Peter and John, who were born and brought up in the capital. They led very cosmopolitan lives and travelled a lot. When she and Nick divorced, Sally went back to Australia with the two boys, then eighteen and sixteen. As Sally recalls, 'It was a double shock for them. They not only lost their father, but also the life they knew – friends, school, and so on. They gradually adjusted, found friends and got used to a new school, but it was a difficult time for them.'

Then Sally met David, a widower with two sons, each slightly older than Peter and John respectively, and a daughter, Kate, who is younger. After a while Sally and David decided to marry and eventually Sally and her boys moved in with David and his three children.

We really should have moved to another house, but at the time this was financially impossible and I felt in any case that David's children needed to be in that house. We made sure they all had their own rooms by building on another floor. But neither set of children really understood what life would be like when we all moved in together. It took months of adjustment. They really didn't get on well at first – they accepted each other, but not much else. The one saving grace was that Peter and John loved having a sister. They were absolutely thrilled with her and those three still have the best relationship.

One of the problems she found was that 'they were all so grown up and set in their ways that we had to negotiate a hell of a lot'. Although Peter was younger by a year than Andrew, David's elder son, he'd had more varied life experiences and his expectations were different. As a result, he felt superior. This threatened Andrew and caused trouble. Peter had come on to Andrew's territory and it felt as though he was trying to usurp him – and in a way he was. Graham, David's younger son, dealt with the invasion by ignoring both John and Peter. Kate, however, was not threatened because she was still the baby – more than that, she had two more brothers to spoil her. She was delighted with the new arrangement, which helped Sally greatly. Not only did she have female support, but Kate acted as a safety valve for the two sets of boys and would often stop rows developing by her presence alone.

Of all five children it was, Sally reckons, toughest for Peter, her elder boy. Not only was he used to being the first-born, but after Sally's divorce he had taken on his father's status: he helped with all kinds of responsibilities, financial and otherwise, and did many jobs around the house. Then along came an older brother *and* a stepfather. He was the first to marry and leave home for good. Now both Andrew and Graham are married, and Sally says it is all much easier. Everyone is good friends – on the whole. It took them five hard years to become really comfortable with each other, but the effort has paid off. As Sally says, 'At Graham's wedding last summer, it was wonderful to see them all sitting round chatting together and I felt we had really achieved something.'

In the much-married world of showbusiness step-families are common. The Hollywood children of stars like Elizabeth Taylor are used to a way of life in which half- or stepbrothers and -sisters are the norm and sibling rivalry hardly has a chance to become established before the parental pattern changes again and a new mother or father appears on the scene.

One Hollywood figure who has absorbed several stepchildren into her family is the British actress Jane Seymour. When she married her second husband, businessman David Flynn, she inherited a stepdaughter, Jennifer, from his previous marriage. Seymour and Flynn then had two children of their own, Katie and Sean, who looked upon Jennifer, who was two years older than Katie, as an older sister.

When the marriage broke up and Seymour married James Keach, an actor–director, she inherited another child, from his previous marriage – this time a stepson, Kalen, who is three years older than Jennifer.

Not long ago the family had two recent additions when Seymour gave birth to twin boys, Kristopher and John. Both she and James were delighted, and at the family Christmas last year, there were six children, all of whom seem to have integrated in spite of, in one case, having a different mother and father, in another a different mother and in a third a different father.

Ingrid Bergman was another actress who made a conscious effort to bring her various children together as often as possible. She tells in her autobiograhy how Pia, the daughter from her first marriage to Dr Petter Lindstrom, lived with her father while growing up in Pittsburgh and Salt Lake City and studied at the University of Colorado and Mills College in San Francisco. After graduating at the age of twenty, she married, but remained with her husband for just one year. Pia went to Paris and lived with Ingrid and her third husband, Lars Schmidt, for six months, then found an apartment of her own. All the time she had been searching fruitlessly for a worthwhile job. Eventually she decided, with her mother's encouragement, to go to Rome to look after Ingrid's children Robin, and twins Ingrid and Isabella (who was later to become a world-famous model and actress) from her second marriage, to Roberto Rossellini. There had been so many dramas and fights over the custody of these children that Bergman had opted to forfeit her claim for the sake of the children's wellbeing. Instead Ingrid travelled to Rome every month for a week or ten days to see them.

Rossellini was often away, and they were living alone with a cook and a nurse when Pia arrived. Ingrid sent Pia money to pay the salaries, and she stayed there for three years, taking the children to the dentist, to lessons, horse-riding, skiing and generally organizing the family. When she left Robin was seventeen and the girls almost fifteen. She says: 'It was a very good experience because in a sense I needed it. I really didn't have a place: I wasn't married; I was at a loose end. I couldn't figure out a profession that I was capable of doing. I really needed roots and a place to live, a feeling that I was functioning, helping somebody and doing something that was necessary.' While she was in Rome she got to know Rossellini: how egocentric but charming he was; how irresponsible yet interesting. The other Rossellini children were daily visitors: son Renzo by his first wife and his two children, Raffaella and Gil, by his third. Pia, who had been brought up as an only child, says, 'I liked my "Italian period" because I had been alone and had a kind of isolated upbringing. This whole atmosphere, this chaotic thing, was very appealing. There was something fascinating about all of us children being together even though the parents were off doing something else.'

Pia had planned to stay in Italy, but was offered a job in America which involved promoting a car on television and radio. It seemed an opportunity not to be missed, and she progressed to working in television in San Francisco, where her father lived, and then in New York, where she became very successful.

Step-families may be on the increase because of the rising divorce rate, but they were common in the past, too, for a different reason. Until the beginning of this century, so many women died in childbirth, or from infections following childbirth, that second and third marriages abounded. As we have already seen, Robert Graves, the writer and poet, had half-siblings; another writer, George Eliot, the author of *Middlemarch* and *The Mill on the Floss*, came from a second family.

Her father, Robert Evans, had married Harriet Poynton in 1801, with two children resulting: Robert, born in 1802, followed by Fanny three years later. Harriet died in 1809 while giving birth prematurely to her third child. In 1813 Evans married Christiana Pearson, who was considered his social superior because her father was a churchwarden. She gave birth to three children, Christiana in 1814, Isaac in 1816 and Mary Anne (George Eliot's real name) in 1819. A highly efficient, disciplined and cold woman, Christiana gave Mary Anne little affection, but the child was close to her father, an estate manager, who would take her on his rounds, when the tenants made a great fuss of her. The five children divided naturally into two groups. In his biography, Frederick Karl says Robert was ready for work and Fanny almost ready for marriage when Mary Anne was born.

So Mary Anne spent most of her time with her full siblings. She later described her early relationship with her brother Isaac as being of more importance to her than any other, except possibly that with her father. Isaac was generally thought to be the model for Tom Tulliver in *The Mill on the Floss*, whom the heroine Maggie wants to play with her, protect and love her.

As the youngest, Mary Anne was quite precocious and her father appreciated his clever daughter. When her mother died, she became the 'wife', her half-sister Fanny having by then married and her sister Chrissy having found work in another town. She loved looking after her father, but as she got older their views began to diverge. She became convinced that a moral life could be led without formal religious worship, having observed the Dissenters, who, she noted, were far more involved in helping the poor and eradicating illiteracy than Church of England worshippers like her father. Her strong social conscience is much in evidence in *Middlemarch*, when Dorothea Brooks puts forward her plan of new homes for the farmworkers.

Concluding that there was little point in continuing to go to church, she told her father that she had decided to stop. Her father drafted in the family to help persuade her back into the fold. Her half-brother Robert warned her she must become dutiful or face censure; her half-sister Fanny said she should put up a good front and comply, and privately keep her own beliefs, just as she, Fanny, did. It hurt most that Isaac told her she would become a pariah and never snare a husband. She refused to submit, but later a compromise was reached and she did once again go to church with her father, keeping her beliefs to herself.

When he died, still displeased at her rejection of the church, he left Mary Anne some money, but bequeathed the set of Scott, which she had read to him when he was dying, and the family silver to Fanny. This upset her. Moving to London, she began working on the liberal Whig *Westminster Review*, which was owned by a friend, John Chapman. One of the contributors was George Lewes. He was at the time in an 'open' marriage – his wife had given birth to four of his children and four fathered by his colleague Thornton Hunts. Lewes had gradually come to find the 'arrangement' unsatisfactory, and soon after he met Mary Ann (she had dropped the 'e' by then), he left his wife and set up home with her. Mary Ann wrote to tell Fanny, her half-sister, with whom she had a good big sister–surrogate-mother relationship, about Lewes, but she disguised the fact that they were not married by signing the letter 'Marian Lewes'. Fanny responded warmly. At the same time she mentioned that a 'Mr Liggin' (the first of Eliot's aliases) had been writing stories about their childhood homes. Mary Ann had also written to Isaac to tell him about Lewes and ask him to have her money paid into Lewes's account at the Union Bank of London. Isaac guessed the true situation and was furious. He put pressure on both Fanny and Chrissy to sever all correspondence with their wayward sister.

These divisions and fears which split her life were underscored in the sonnet sequence, 'Brother and Sister', which she wrote in 1869, when she was starting *Middlemarch*. She seems to have been seeking a reunion with Isaac, though the sonnet reveals uncertainty, ambiguity and some hostility.

Lewes was unable to get a divorce from his wife because he had condoned her adultery by adopting the first child fathered by Hunt. So Lewes and Mary Ann were doomed to 'live in sin', as it was then considered. Even with the success of *Middlemarch* the family remained unforgiving. By then, Isaac was fifty-six and Fanny sixty-seven. George Eliot, as she had now become, had no children of her own but became very close to her stepchildren, particularly Charles and Bertie. When Lewes died she saw a great deal of Charles, his wife and their children (sadly, Bertie had also died).

George Eliot eventually married – when she was almost sixty – to a man in his forties, John Cross. He was more of a worshipper or disciple than a husband, but he cared for her devotedly in their short marriage – she died within eighteen months – and later wrote a biography of her.

The burden can be very heavy at times for half- or stepbrothers and -sisters, but when the families have settled down and feel more comfortable with each other, it can sometimes be an advantage to have additional siblings with whom to form relationships, and two sets of parents to take care of you.

It seems that, in spite of displacement, step-families can work, providing the initial parental input is understanding enough. Certainly, jealousy, resentment and total incompatibility do provide major problems, but even these can be resolved with determination and patience.

Conclusion

Although I have tried to select case histories from as wide a range of families as possible, even a much longer study could not hope to cover their infinite variety. The number of potential permutations, taking into account such factors as the balance of boys and girls or the age gaps within families, is almost infinite. It could make a substantial difference that the first-born is a boy rather than a girl, though normally it does not; or three children born at five-year intervals may feel like so many only children. Generally, however, a more typical pattern of relationships will evolve.

Equally, economic factors may play a large part in a family's experience. Again, the possible permutations are endless. The parents may be comfortably off when the first-born arrives, but impoverished by the time the fifth appears on the scene, or vice versa. With today's job insecurities, changes can be terribly swift.

Early this century B. S. Rowntree made a study of poverty. In it he showed how the family circle worked from an economic point of view. The financial status of the family diminished with the arrival of each child, so that the last-born had fewer advantages than the first, and it remained low until the children were of working age, at which point the family income increased and stayed high until the children left home. The remainder of the family was then left in reduced circumstances again. This study was based on the British working-class family, but later studies have confirmed that Rowntree's findings were not restricted to the working classes. There may be other influences, of course: the role of head of the family or breadwinner might be thrust on the first-born because of death or recession, or the last left in the parental home may have to be the carer in the case of parental illness. Yet despite these caveats, we have seen the emergence – or confirmation – of what look like fairly clear patterns of experience affecting each place in the family. To summarize what has been covered in each chapter:

- First-borns start off with the benefits of being an only child. They compensate for their subsequent dethronement by striving to meet their parents' high expectations and to regain their pole position.
- The second child is likely to rebel against parental authority and the 'goody two-shoes' elder sibling. This rebellion may take a creative form; it may result in the child being laid back to the point of idleness.
- The middle child can have a tough time, enjoying no clear status and searching for a role. With three children, it helps greatly if the older and younger siblings are of the opposite sex.
- The youngest is luckiest. He or she has plenty of attention from parents and siblings alike. Too much spoiling can, however, totally undermine motivation.

- The only child risks being parent-bound and is likely to be precocious and self-sufficient. School may seem a tough environment. Early flight from parental claustrophobia is possible.
- Children in large families may lack parental attention. In compensation, they have the company and support of their siblings and a strong sense of tribal solidarity.
- Twins, especially identical twins, may initially enjoy their unique status and rapport with their 'other half'. But as they grow older they face the difficult task of establishing their own identity.
- Adopted children are vulnerable, especially if they are brought up with the biological children of their adoptive parents. Some decide to seek out their birth mothers, others fear the potential consequences of doing so.
- Stepchildren run the risk of disliking, and being disliked by, their step-parent and of being ousted from their familiar place by stepbrothers and -sisters.

No one should underestimate the deep desire of every child for the *exclusive* love of his or her parents. Learning to share that love is one of the earliest lessons in life. Yet it is possible within the family to satisfy that desire in each child to be wanted, to be understood, to be appreciated and to be loved. That love, emanating from siblings as well as parents, creates the bonds that bind a child emotionally to its family. Nowhere else can the child and the emerging adult find that unique sense of social and biological identity, as Bossard and Boll have pointed out. Even the happiest adopted children often seek out their birth parents – they have their social identity, but their biological dimension is missing.

I hope readers will enjoy comparing their own experiences of family relationships with those described in these pages. Perhaps they will see their own place in the pecking order in a new light; perhaps they will be comforted to discover how much more difficult others have found a similar position. Although all generalizations must be treated with suspicion, one thing is certain: family life is never static. I hope this book has pinned down a few recurring elements in its ever-changing drama.

Bibliography

Adler, A.: *What Life Should Mean to You* (Allen & Unwin, 1932).

Adler, A.: *Social Interest* (Faber & Faber, 1938).

Beauman, N.: *E. M. Forster: A Biography* (Hodder & Stoughton, 1993).

Bedser, A. with Bannister, A.: *Twin Ambitions: An autobiography* (Stanley Paul, 1986).

Beer, W. R.: *Strangers in the House* (Transaction Publishers, 1989).

Bergman, I., with Burgess, A.: *My Story* (Michael Joseph, 1980).

Bills, P.: *Carling: A Man Apart* (Victor Gollancz, 1993).

Bossard, J. and Boll, E. S.: *The Sociology of Child Development* (Harper & Row, 1948).

Bowlby, J.: *A Secure Base* (Basic Books, 1988).

Boycott, G.: *An Autobiography* (Macmillan, 1987).

Collier, P. and Horowitz, D.: *The Kennedys* (Secker & Warburg, 1985).

Cooper, H.: *H. for 'Enry: More Than Just an Autobiography* (Collins/Fontana, 1994).

Cosgrave, P.: *The Lives of Enoch Powell* (The Bodley Head, 1989).

De-la-Noy, M.: *Elgar: The Man* (Allen Lane, 1983).

Duvall, E. M.: *Family Development* (J. Lippincott, 1957).

Ellis, N. Wyn: *John Major* (Macdonald, 1991).

Ellman, R.: *Oscar Wilde* (Hamish Hamilton, 1987).

Faldo, N. with Critchley, B.: *Faldo* (Weidenfeld & Nicolson, 1994).

Festing, S.: *A Life of Forms* (Viking, 1995).

Freud, S.: *The Psychopathology of Everyday Life* (Penguin, 1985).

Gilbert, M.: *Churchill: A Life* (Heinemann, 1991).

Junor, P.: *Wife, Mother, Politician* (Sidgwick & Jackson, 1983).

Karl, F.: *George Eliot* (HarperCollins, 1995).

Kiernan, T.: *The Life of Laurence Olivier* (Sidgwick & Jackson, 1981).

Koch, H. L.: *Family Constellation Characteristics* (Child Development, 1955).

Lewis, R.: *Margaret Thatcher* (Routledge & Kegan Paul, 1975).

Longford, E.: *The Pebbled Shore* (Weidenfeld & Nicolson, 1986).

Major-Ball, T.: *Major Major* (Duckworth, 1994).

McDermott, P.: *Sister and Brothers* (Lowell House, 1994).

Mittler, P.: *The Study of Twins* (Penguin Science of Behaviour, 1971).

Moore, B. with Jones, S.: *Brian Moore* (Transworld, 1995).

Parkinson, C.: *Right at the Centre* (Weidenfeld & Nicolson, 1992).

Parsons, T.: *George Michael Bare* (Michael Joseph, 1990).

Pitkeathley, J. and Emerson, D.: *Only Child* (Souvenir Press, 1994).

Robinson, D.: *Chaplin: His Life and Art* (Paladin, 1986).

Seymour-Smith, M.: *Robert Graves* (Hutchinson, 1982).

Stanford, P.: *Lord Longford: An Authorised Life* (Heine-mann, 1994).

Stewart, L.: *Changemakers* (Routledge, 1985).

Sutton-Smith, B. and Rosenberg, B.: *The Sibling* (Holt, Rinehart and Winston Inc., 1970).

Toman, W.: *Family Constellation: Its Effect on Person-ality and Social Behaviour* (Springer, 1976).

Wallace, M.: *The Silent Twins* (Penguin, 1994).

Other Sources

Australian Good Weekend, Bronwyn Donaghy, June 1995.

Evening Standard, Madeleine Harper, September 1993.

Evening Standard, Suzie Mackenzie, April 1995.

The Sunday Times Magazine, 'Relative Values' feature, January 1990, September 1992, February 1993.

National Foundation for Education Research
Parent to Parent Information on Adoption Service